unicorn

unicorn

Belinda Ray

SCHOLASTIC INC.
New York Toronto London Auckland Sydney
Mexico City New Delhi Hong Kong Buenos Aires

ISBN 0-439-56012-8

Copyright © 2003 17th Street Productions,
an Alloy company
All rights reserved.
Published by Scholastic Inc.

 Produced by 17th Street Productions,
an Alloy company
151 West 26th Street
New York, NY 10001

12 11 10 9 8 7 6 5   4 5 6 7 8/0

Printed in the U.S.A.   40
First printing, November 2003

unicorn

CHAPTER
One

"Class, I have a special announcement to make," Mrs. Wessex said first thing Monday morning. The room went silent, and Carrie Weingarten glanced at her friends.

From her seat two rows over, Anna Lee just shrugged. She was too new to Elizabeth Cady Stanton Middle School to understand that Mrs. Wessex's special announcements were indeed *special*.

Theresa Allen, who sat right in front of Carrie, turned and grinned. *"Another tepee?"* she whispered, her brown eyes lighting up. Carrie smiled.

Last month, when they'd been studying Native Americans, Mrs. Wessex's "special announcement" had been that they were going to build a full-size tepee in the classroom. It had been awesome.

First they'd hiked through the woods behind the school to gather fallen birch limbs. Next they'd stripped off the bark, brought the branches inside, lashed them together, and covered them with pieces of leather donated by a local tannery. Then they'd painted the outside with Native American designs.

When it was finished, the tepee had taken up an entire corner of the room. It was large enough to fit about eight people inside at a time. Mrs. Wessex had divided the class into a bunch of different tribes that were native to New England, and each tribe had gotten their own day to "live" in the tepee.

Another one of those would be cool, Carrie thought. Or maybe some kind of pyramid, since they'd been studying ancient Egypt. *Or a model of the Sphinx or Cleopatra's barge . . .*

"It's time for us to start working on the annual fifth-grade production," Mrs. Wessex announced, interrupting Carrie's guessing game.

There were a few squeals of excitement around the room and a couple of "cools" tossed out, but all Carrie could do was blink.

"Already?" she murmured to Theresa. "I thought the fifth-grade musical was usually in the spring."

"Take a look outside," Theresa whispered back.

Carrie gazed out the window, surprised to see just one small mound of snow remaining at the edge of the parking lot. The rest of it was gone. Apparently, all the wet weather they'd had over the last few weeks—along with the milder temperatures—had melted the snow away.

It was still gray outside, but it didn't look cold anymore. There were even a few patches of grass on the front lawn that had started to turn from dead winter tan to vibrant spring green.

Okay, so maybe the *weather* was ready for the fifth-grade play, but Carrie still wasn't—even though she'd been waiting five years for it.

When Carrie was in kindergarten, her older sister, Lynn, had worked as a stagehand in *her* fifth-grade production of *Alice in Wonderland*. Mrs. Hendrickson, the music teacher, had allowed Carrie to sit backstage and help Lynn with props and costumes.

It had been love at first sight. Everything about the theater fascinated Carrie. Just standing *near* the stage made her giddy with excitement. But then after the final performance of *Alice in Wonderland*—the Sunday matinee—Carrie had walked out onstage to help take down the set and looked out at where the audience had been. And her heart leaped in her chest. It was then that she knew where she really belonged: not behind the stage but *on it*. Later that night she'd told her parents that she wanted to be an actress when she grew up. And now, in fifth grade, it was still true.

Carrie loved to sing and dance, and she could recite entire movie scenes from memory. But it wasn't just that she enjoyed all of those things: She was actually good at them.

At least, she was good at acting . . . *in front of the mirror*. And she was good at singing . . . *in the shower*. And dancing? She was the star of the family room . . . *when it was empty*. But give her an audience, and she fell apart.

Only a few days ago she'd nearly fainted giving a presentation on King Tut. She'd had it down pat the night before. But the minute she'd had to stand up in front of the class, her mind had gone blank, her knees had gone weak, and her mouth had gone stupid.

If I can't even do a stupid two-minute oral report, how am I ever going to perform onstage? Carrie wondered. She took a deep breath and tried to steady her nerves. After all, it wasn't like she had to do anything today. Mrs. Wessex had just made the announcement. They probably still had a week or so to read over parts and decide what they wanted to audition for.

Maybe if Carrie could practice in advance and really perfect one of the parts, she'd be able to work up the courage to do it in front of others. And really, she *had* to. It was the only way her dream of acting was ever going to come true.

Okay, she told herself, feeling a bit calmer. *It's all right. I've got time. I can do this.*

"What's the play, Mrs. Wessex?" Maria Mancini asked.

"We've chosen a modern version of *Cinderella,*" Mrs. Wessex said. "I think it should be a lot of fun."

"Cinderella," Sharon Ross repeated. "She has long blonde hair, right?" She flipped her own long blonde hair over her shoulder as she spoke.

Theresa mimicked her, throwing a few braids over her shoulder prima-donna style. Unfortunately, her hair was so long that it smacked Carrie in the face.

"Hey!" Carrie hissed, but Theresa just giggled.

"Not always," Anna said.

"What was that, Anna?" Mrs. Wessex asked.

"Oh, I just meant that Cinderella doesn't always have blonde hair," Anna said. "My grandmother has a book of old fairy tales from different cultures, and there's an Egyptian Cinderella with black hair and dark eyes."

Sharon scowled in Anna's direction, but Carrie and Theresa grinned.

"Love her," Theresa whispered, and Carrie nodded in agreement. Anna definitely had a talent for putting Sharon in her place.

"That's an excellent point, Anna," Mrs. Wessex said. "And you're right. Cinderella certainly doesn't have to have blonde hair."

"Hey—if it's a modern fairy tale, maybe she could have a shaved head," Jeremy Gray suggested.

"Or purple hair," Billy Rafuse added.

"Well, I'm not sure about that," Mrs. Wessex said, "but it's certainly open to interpretation. In any case, Mrs. Hendrickson and I will be holding the auditions tomorrow during your music period—right after lunch."

Tomorrow?! Carrie swallowed hard. Couldn't Mrs. Wessex have given them a little more notice? How on earth was she supposed to pick a part, get it right, and work up enough confidence to audition in just one day?

Forget it, Carrie thought. *I'm doomed.*

"Mrs. Wessex?"

It was Sharon again. She probably wanted to mention that she'd been thinking of shaving her head. Or dyeing her hair purple. Or black. Just in case. Carrie glanced over at Anna, who rolled her eyes.

"Yes, Sharon?"

"I was just wondering, do you have any music we should study overnight? Or maybe some lines we should memorize to prepare for the audition?"

Mrs. Wessex's eyes widened. "Well, that's quite industrious of you, Sharon, but no, you don't need to prepare anything," she said. "We'll read over the script this afternoon so everyone gets a feel for it. Tonight I'd just like everyone to think about what they might like to do for the play, whether it's acting, helping to design the set, working on costumes, lighting, sound, programs, tickets, advertising—there's a lot to be done. There should be something for everyone."

The class buzzed with excitement as everyone started talking about which jobs they wanted.

"Quiet, please," Mrs. Wessex said, raising one hand in the air and holding it there until the voices died down. "Now, anyone who wants to try out for a part can sign up tomorrow morning in class. I'll have sign-up sheets for all the other jobs, too, and we'll talk about the work involved in each one."

"I want a part," Carrie heard Maria whisper to Lauren Graham.

"Me too," Lauren replied.

Ugh. Carrie's stomach dropped. Everyone was going to be trying out for parts, and they were all bound to be better than she was. Not that it would be difficult. All they had to do was speak. It was more than Carrie could manage.

"Oh, and I almost forgot," Mrs. Wessex added. "I have another announcement to make." She retrieved a piece of paper from her desk and read it aloud. "Tomorrow we'll be welcoming a new student to our class. Ward Willis is transferring from Kennebunk Elementary School. I expect everyone to give him a warm welcome."

Anna gave a silent clap as she looked over at Theresa and Carrie. "I'm not the new kid anymore!" she mouthed.

Carrie smiled back at her. She'd stopped thinking of Anna as the new kid a while ago. It had only been a couple of weeks, but it already felt like they'd been friends for a long time.

In fact, the other day, when Carrie had botched her King Tut presentation, it had been Anna who'd tried to help her. She'd noticed that Carrie was feeling pretty down and loaned her a charm bracelet, saying it had brought her good luck once.

Carrie looked down at her wrist. She touched the silver angel charm and ran her fingers along the cool metal chain. Unfortunately, something told her it was going to take more than good luck to get her a role in the play. It was going to take a miracle.

CHAPTER
Two

"The play sounds pretty cool, huh?" Anna said as she joined Carrie and Theresa at their usual table in the cafeteria.

"Yeah," Theresa agreed. "I can't wait to sign up. What are you guys going to do?"

"I was thinking about helping with the ticket and program design," Anna said. "I kind of like fooling around on my computer with that stuff."

"Cool," Theresa said. "I was thinking costumes and props. And maybe set design, too—I'm not sure. I wonder how many committees we can sign up for."

"I don't know," Anna said. "What about you, Carrie? What are you going to do?"

"Huh? Oh, I—I'm not sure," Carrie stammered. She wasn't quite ready to admit that she wanted to audition for a part. It was as if she said it out loud, she'd have to go through with it. And no matter how much she wanted to, she wasn't sure she had the nerve. So instead she decided to focus on something less frightening—her lunch. Unfortunately, these days it was only *slightly* less frightening.

Her father had been on a major health kick lately, and more and more it was making its way into Carrie's reusable canvas lunch bag. She unrolled the top of it carefully and peered inside.

Hmmm. Not bad, Carrie thought, removing the contents—a veggie wrap, wheat crackers with hummus, and carob chip cookies for dessert.

"Whoa—your dad's slipping," Theresa commented. "That actually looks edible. And he packed cookies."

"Frookies," Carrie corrected her.

"Frookies?" Anna and Theresa repeated together.

"Yeah. They're sweetened with fruit juice instead of sugar," Carrie explained. "But you're right," she added, looking down at her spread. "This actually looks pretty good. Way better than yesterday's tofu-pineapple pie."

Anna shuddered. "No offense to your father, Carrie, but that was gross. Even my brother wouldn't have eaten it, and he eats everything."

"No one would eat it," Carrie said. "Not even

Dad. My mom made him throw it away last night and promise never to make it again."

"Whoa," Theresa said. "It must have been bad for your mom to say that. She's usually so mellow."

"It was the worst, Theresa," Anna said. "I had a bite, remember? It was *sooo* gross. I told Matt about it in the arcade yesterday, and he said it sounded like one of the rogues from Storm Ranger."

Theresa raised her eyebrows. "There's a tofu-pineapple monster in Storm Ranger?"

"No," Anna said, "but there *is* a warrior that started out as a leftover bowl of seafood stew and mutated."

Carrie and Theresa stared at Anna with narrowed eyes.

"Really," Anna insisted. "He's called Bouillabeast." There was a moment's hesitation, and then all three girls burst out laughing.

"What's so funny?" someone asked.

Carrie turned to see Sharon approaching with Kimberly Price close behind. Sharon sat next to Carrie, and Kimberly took the seat next to her.

"We were just talking about Carrie's lunch," Theresa explained.

"Oh," Sharon said, glancing toward Carrie's food. "Whoa, Carrie—your dad packed cookies? What's up with that?"

"He's trying to make up for the fact that yesterday's lunch was an evil mutant bent on destroying the world," Anna said with a completely straight face. Again she, Theresa, and Carrie stared at one another for a moment . . . and then burst out laughing.

"I'm not even going to ask." Sharon shook her head. She took the small plastic cup of pasta sauce on her tray and poured it over her spaghetti. "So," she said, twirling some pasta around her fork, "have you guys thought about the play at all? Do you know what you're going to do?"

Carrie's smile disappeared. Why did everyone have to keep bringing up the stupid play?

"Costumes and props," Theresa answered right away. "And maybe set design. I'm hoping Mrs. Wessex will let me sign up for both."

"What about you, Lee?" Sharon asked. She always called Anna by her last name.

"I'm not sure," Anna said. "I *was* thinking ticket and program design, but set design sounds pretty cool, too. I think I might sign up for that."

"Really?" Theresa grinned. "That would be awesome." She glanced at Carrie and then back to Anna. "Then all three of us could work together."

Carrie narrowed her eyes. "All three of us?" she asked.

Anna smiled. "Yeah, that's what I was thinking, too. Wouldn't that be great?"

"Well . . . yeah, but . . ." Carrie wasn't sure what to say. "I, uh, haven't actually decided what I want to do yet."

"Really?" Theresa asked. "I just assumed you'd want to do set design because you're such a good artist."

"Yeah," Anna agreed. "That's what I figured, too. You draw so well."

"Oh," Carrie said. "Thanks. Well, I *might* do that, but—"

"At least we all know you're not trying out for a part," Kimberly said with a chortle.

Carrie's heart skipped. What was *that* supposed to mean? She looked to Theresa and Anna, surprised to see them both gazing back at her with . . . *pity*? Was that what it was? Carrie didn't know what to say, and apparently nobody else did, either. They'd all gone silent, and now everyone was staring at Kimberly.

"What?" Kimberly said. "I wasn't trying to be *mean*." She looked at Carrie. "I just meant . . .

well . . . you know . . . remember your Egypt presentation? *Ting Kut?*"

Carrie winced.

"It just seems obvious that you don't like standing up in front of people," Kimberly added. "That's all I meant. Not that you couldn't do it or anything."

"Right," Theresa jumped in. "I mean, I'm sure you *could* if you wanted to." She paused to glance at Anna. "Right?"

"Definitely," Anna said, nodding.

"We just didn't think you'd want to," Theresa went on. "And . . . you don't . . . *do you?*"

Carrie felt all of her friends' eyes on her while they waited for her reaction. She also felt her cheeks growing hot and knew they were turning a shade of red to match her hair. It didn't exactly seem like the right time to admit that she dreamed of being onstage—especially because clearly none of her friends thought she'd be good at it. They were obviously only saying that other stuff to avoid hurting her feelings.

"I don't know," she finally managed. "Probably not." Everyone seemed to relax at those two words. Everyone except Carrie. "Anyway, I know what you meant, Kimberly," Carrie went on.

"And you're right—I do get nervous talking in front of people."

"Who doesn't?" Kimberly said. "I hate oral reports."

"Me too," agreed Theresa.

"I don't," Sharon said. "I got over stage fright a long time ago."

"Stage fright?" Carrie repeated.

"Yeah, that's what it's called when you get scared about performing in front of other people."

"Oh," Carrie said. "Right." She picked up a wheat cracker and dipped it into the hummus. Maybe Sharon was trying to be helpful, but somehow having a name for her fear made it seem that much more real.

Sharon picked up a forkful of spaghetti but stopped just short of shoving it into her mouth. "Hey—you know what?" she said, gesturing at Carrie with her overloaded utensil.

"What?" Carrie asked.

"You *should* try out for a part."

Carrie nearly choked on her cracker. "I *what*?"

Sharon chewed her pasta, then dabbed at her mouth with her napkin. "You should try out for a part," she repeated. Everyone, including Carrie, stared at Sharon in surprise.

"I'm serious," Sharon insisted. "If you have

stage fright, the only way to get over it is to confront it. That's what my drama coach always says."

"Your *drama coach*?" Anna asked.

"Mm-hm," Sharon replied, twirling another strand of spaghetti onto her fork. "I take jazz, ballet, and acting classes, and my drama coach, Ms. Harkins, is always telling new students that if they want to get over stage fright, they just have to get up and perform. And it's true. After a while you get so used to being in front of people that it's not scary at all anymore."

"Really?" Carrie asked. She glanced at Anna and Theresa for their reactions. They both raised their eyebrows and shrugged. Obviously, they were just as puzzled as Carrie was. Not only was Sharon offering advice, she actually seemed to be offering *good* advice—without a selfish reason in sight.

"Sure," Sharon said. "Plus I already talked with Mrs. Wessex about the play. There's the lead role, Cindy Rellar, which I'll probably get, and then there are a bunch of supporting parts. If you tried for one of those, you wouldn't have to be onstage all that much, and when you are, I could help you out. I'd probably be out there, too—you know, because the lead gets the most stage time."

Okay. Now that sounded a little more like Sharon. But overall, the advice was good.

"Thanks," Carrie said. "I'll think about it."

"You should," Sharon said. "There are a lot of little parts to fill. Just about everybody who tries out is sure to get something. And who knows? If you get a small enough role, you might be able to work on set design, too."

"That would be perfect," Theresa said.

"Yeah," Anna agreed. "Then you'd get a chance to get over your stage fright and the three of us could still work together. Wouldn't that be great?"

"Yeah. Great," Carrie said, forcing a smile. A *little part* would be okay, but it wasn't exactly what she'd had in mind. She wanted a lead role—like the one Sharon was trying out for—but no one else seemed to think that she could handle it.

And, unfortunately, Carrie had a feeling they were right.

CHAPTER
Three

"Can we do Sound Factory next?" Carrie asked as she and Theresa passed through the food court at the mall. "The new Strawberries and Cream CD came out this weekend, and I really want to get it."

"Okay," Theresa said, "but Sara's is on the way, so let's stop in there first."

Carrie groaned. Sara's was the accessory store, and—in Carrie's mind—one of the most boring stores in the entire mall. She squinted at Theresa. "Do you really need another hair clip?" she asked.

"Do you really need another CD?" Theresa shot back.

Carrie rolled her eyes. "All right," she said with a sigh, "but just for a minute, okay? I don't want to spend the whole afternoon looking at barrettes and bracelets."

"I'll be quick," Theresa said with a big grin. When they reached Sara's, she bounced into the store and headed straight for the hair accessories. Carrie shuffled in behind her, stopping to browse through a spinning rack of sunglasses. She pulled out the ugliest pair she could find— bright purple rims with neon green lenses—and tried them on.

"What do you think, Resa?" she asked.

Theresa glanced up and grimaced. "Definitely a fashion *don't*," she answered, shaking her head. Then, without so much as a smirk, she went back to rummaging through the clips, combs, and barrettes.

Carrie frowned. It was too bad Anna hadn't been able to come. She wasn't into accessorizing any more than Carrie was. Theresa, on the other hand, was always trying to get the two of them to put their hair up and wear a little lip gloss. "It's fun," she was constantly telling them and "It'll make you feel older," to which Anna had once replied, "So will wearing my grandmother's false teeth, but I'm not trying those on, either."

Carrie smiled. If Anna had been there, she would have laughed at the ugly purple-and-green glasses and then tried to find something even worse. Unfortunately, she'd had to go to the dentist, and her mother hadn't been considerate enough to make the appointment during school hours.

"Hey—how about this?" Theresa asked, holding up a green hair clip shaped like a big butterfly.

Carrie shrugged. "It's okay," she said, "but it doesn't really look like you."

"It's not *for* me," Theresa said. "It's for you." Carrie rolled her eyes. "Oh, come on, Car—it would be perfect. This bright green clip in your dark red hair? It would be so sweet. Plus it would help you to keep some of that hair out of your face."

"Thanks, but no thanks," Carrie said, even though her bangs were hanging down over her eyes and she had to keep brushing them away. A clip actually would be a big help while she was growing them out, but she kind of liked the way the curls hid her face. Besides, she didn't want to encourage Theresa by giving in.

Theresa sighed and put the clip back in its bin, then moved on to jewelry.

Carrie walked over to join her. "Are you almost ready?" she asked.

"Just about. Ooh—look at that." Theresa reached for a necklace at the top of the jewelry stand, stretching her hand up. "Oh, no—oops!"

There was a loud crash as Theresa knocked over a whole rack of earrings. They clattered across the floor and under tables, and everyone turned to stare. Blushing, Theresa quickly knelt down to start picking up the earrings. In a flash, one of the store clerks was beside her.

"You can just leave them there," the clerk said, glaring at Theresa. "I'll take care of it."

"I—I'm sorry," Theresa said, still trying to scoop up all the earrings.

The clerk placed her hand on top of Theresa's. "Miss, really—just leave them there," she said. Her tone was short and clipped.

"Okay, but . . . I'm *really* sorry," Theresa repeated, stepping away.

"Mm-hm," the clerk mumbled, without looking up. As Carrie and Theresa left, she muttered something about irresponsible kids and needing to get a new job.

"Jeez. She didn't have to be so mean about it," Theresa said when they were safely out of earshot. "It was just an accident."

"I know," Carrie said. "Don't worry about it." She felt bad for Theresa. Stuff like that was always happening to her—spilling food, knocking over huge displays, tripping over things. It had to be embarrassing. *Kind of like standing up to give a report on King Tut and freezing.* Carrie snorted at the thought.

"What?" Theresa asked.

"Oh, nothing. I was just thinking about my King Tut presentation."

"Kimberly really wasn't trying to be mean at lunch today, you know," Theresa said.

"I know," Carrie said. And she did—but that didn't mean it hadn't hurt.

The two girls walked silently past a nutrition store and a pet store, two shoe stores, and a gift shop, and before Carrie knew it, they were just outside Sound Factory. Theresa started in, but Carrie caught her by the elbow. "Hey," she said, pulling Theresa aside. "Do you think Sharon was right?"

"About what?"

"About stage fright. You know, today at lunch when she said all that stuff about just getting up and performing?"

Theresa shrugged. "I don't know. I guess so. I mean, that's kind of like what my dad always tells me. *'You have to face your fears, Theresa,'*" she said in a deep, fatherly voice. "Of course, he's usually talking about trying whatever strange vegetable is on my dinner plate, but I guess it could work for other stuff. Why?"

Carrie bit her lip. "Well . . . *because.*"

"Because *why*?"

"Because . . ." Carrie took a deep breath. She had to tell someone, and Theresa was her closest friend. "Because . . . I think I want to try out," she blurted. "For the play."

Theresa blinked. "Really?"

Carrie winced. *Oh, no.* It was true. Theresa didn't think she could do it. Her best friend, who knew her better than anyone else in the world, didn't think she could—

"That would be awesome," Theresa said, breaking into a big grin. "It would be so cool to see you onstage."

Carrie's jaw dropped. "Really?" she asked.

"Absolutely." Theresa nodded. "And you know what? You'd be great—I can totally see you up there."

"You can?"

"Yeah."

"Am I talking? Or am I just staring out at the audience like an idiot?"

Theresa clucked her tongue. "*Carrie,*" she said. "Of course you're talking. And you're singing and dancing, too. And the audience is clapping like crazy."

Carrie smiled. It was a nice image. She'd pictured herself onstage thousands of times, and she'd never frozen in her imagination, either. "Wow," she murmured. "That would be so great." She squinted at Theresa, trying to determine whether her friend was being honest or just nice. "So . . . you *really* think I should audition?" she asked.

"Definitely," Theresa said.

Hmmm. No hesitation, direct eye contact, Carrie assessed. Theresa seemed to mean it. And Sharon had seemed sincere when she'd suggested Carrie try out at lunch. *So maybe,* Carrie thought, *just maybe I should.* It was simply a matter of working up the nerve.

"Hey," Theresa said, glancing over Carrie's shoulder. "There's your sister."

Carrie turned and saw her older sister, Lynn, and Lynn's best friend, Stephanie Lane, walking out of Maxine's. Each of them was carrying a large double-handled shopping bag.

Maybe they won't notice us, Carrie thought. She'd had enough of her sister during the car ride to the mall.

It wasn't that she and Lynn didn't get along, exactly. It was just that they rarely agreed. On anything. And Carrie didn't feel like arguing with her sister in the middle of the mall.

Unfortunately, Theresa didn't notice that

Carrie was more or less hiding behind a potted palm. Theresa cupped her hands around her mouth and called, "Hey, Lynn!" Lynn looked up, waved, and headed their way.

"Check out this skirt," Lynn said, pulling a multicolored miniwrap out of her bag. "And I got this top to match. Maxine's is having such a great sale. You two should really check it out."

"Nice," Theresa said. "Maybe we will." She glanced at Carrie, but Carrie only shrugged.

"I just want to hit Sound Factory," she said. "After that, I don't care."

"That's my sister," Lynn said. "Always blowing all of her money on CDs."

"What's wrong with that?" Carrie said.

"Nothing," Lynn admitted. "Except that you never have any cool clothes to wear and you're always begging to borrow mine."

"I don't beg to borrow—"

"Hey—guess what?" Theresa cut in.

Carrie frowned. She knew Theresa hated to watch her and her sister fight, but did she always have to interrupt just when Carrie was about to put her sister in her place?

"What?" Lynn asked.

"Mrs. Wessex told us today that the class play is going to be a modern version of *Cinderella*,"

Theresa blathered, "and Carrie's going to try out for a part."

Carrie's eyebrows shot up. "Theresa!" she hissed. She hadn't meant for it to become headline news.

"You are?" Lynn asked, taking a step back. "Really?" She looked stunned.

"Well . . . I'm thinking about it," Carrie said.

"Huh. I know you wanted to be an actress back when you were like, *six*, but ever since that whole karaoke thing I thought you kind of gave that up. Remember that? You said you were never going to sing in public again."

Carrie cringed. Actually, she'd pretty much forgotten about it. Until now. Leave it to her sister to make matters worse.

"Lynn," Stephanie said, "that was like, your twelfth birthday, wasn't it? Carrie was only eight—she probably doesn't even remember it."

Seven, Carrie thought, *and yes, I do*. It had been one of the most embarrassing moments of her life—one that she had managed to block out . . . up until this very moment.

"What happened?" Theresa asked.

"Oh, my gosh, she never *told you*?" Lynn said. She gaped at Carrie, who scowled back. "Theresa, you *have* to hear this. It's such a funny story."

"It's not funny, Lynn—it's stupid," Carrie said. "And boring. And I'm sure Theresa doesn't want to hear about it."

"Oh yes, I—" Theresa started, then she paused, craning her neck to look over Lynn's shoulder. "Hey, wait—isn't that . . . ? Matt!" she called. "Over here!"

Carrie turned to see Matt Dana walking out of Sound Factory with another boy who she didn't recognize. Oh, great. Just what she needed. A larger audience for her sister's humiliating story.

Gee, Theresa, maybe that old couple on the bench would like to hear it, too. Why don't you call them over? Carrie thought bitterly.

"Hey—Theresa, Carrie, what's up?" Matt said as he approached. Then he nodded to his friend. "This is Ward."

"*MC Spence,*" the boy cut in.

"Oh, right," Matt said. "I forgot. Sorry."

"No worries, man," Matt's friend said. "It's just a name for the rhyming game—I may achieve fame, but I'll remain the same."

Carrie and Theresa—and Lynn and Stephanie— all stared at Matt and . . . *MC Spence.*

"Do people actually *call* you that?" Theresa asked.

"Not yet," Ward said. "I just made it up."

"What does *Spence* mean?" Stephanie asked.

"Nothing. Spencer's my middle name," Ward said.

"Oh," Lynn said, nodding. "So you're . . . *MC Spence*. That's . . . cute."

There was a moment of silence that Carrie noticed seemed to make everyone in the group feel awkward—everyone except Ward, that is. He was rifling through the pockets of his baggy cargo jeans for something. "Cool," he said when he finally pulled out what looked like a piece of lint.

"Anyway, Ward," Matt went on, "I mean, *MC Spence*—is the new kid Mrs. Wessex was talking about. I know him from the skate park."

"Oh, hi," Theresa and Carrie said at just about the same time.

"This is Theresa," Matt continued, "and that's Carrie."

"And this is my sister, Lynn," Carrie said, practically sneering her sister's name, "and her friend, Stephanie."

As everyone said their hellos, Carrie checked out MC Spence. Too bad Anna wasn't here—she'd be psyched to know that not only was she no longer the newest student at ECS, but she was no longer the shortest, either. Or if she was, it wasn't by much. Ward was only about four-six, which would place him right around Anna's height—maybe even an inch below.

He was wearing a black T-shirt that said RAP THIS across the chest, and he had headphones hanging around his neck. Carrie followed the wires to see a Discman clipped onto his side pocket, where she could also see the corner of a Sound Factory bag poking out.

"So," Spence said with a nod, "you guys hang at Elizabeth Cady with Matt?"

"We go there, yeah," Theresa said. "You're starting tomorrow?"

"Yeah, the 'rents got a new place, so I had to switch schools." He shrugged. "It's cool, though, you know? I'll get to chill with my buddy Matt." He pulled the Sound Factory bag from his pocket and took out a CD.

Carrie gasped. "You got the new Strawberries and Cream! Can I see it?"

Spence grinned. "You into them?" he said, handing her the CD.

"I was just on my way to buy it," Carrie answered.

"Cool," Spence said with a nod. "Check it out—there's a new version of 'Pretty Girl' on there."

Carrie flipped the disk over to see all the tracks. "Awesome—it has 'Automatic Focus,' too—I love that song. And it looks like there's a bunch of new stuff." Carrie was just about to ask Spence if he knew anything about the track called "On the Corner of Milk and Market" when she heard her sister sigh.

"Well, Steph and I have to get going," Lynn said. She always made a big show of being bored by Carrie and her "little friends," as Lynn referred to them. "We only have about an hour left, Carrie. Don't forget to meet us at the big clock at four—"

"Forty-five. I know," Carrie said, rolling her eyes. Lynn had reminded her approximately twenty-three times now—as if Carrie was the one who was perpetually late. *Oh, well,* Carrie thought. *At least she's leaving.*

"Wait," Theresa said. "What about the karaoke party? You haven't told me the story yet."

Carrie gave her sister a panicked glance. *Not in front of Matt and his friend,* she thought, hoping that for once her and Lynn's shared genes would aid their communication. But Lynn was clueless. As usual.

"Oh, right," she said. "I almost forgot." It didn't even seem to cross her mind that the story might be embarrassing for Carrie. Or maybe it did, and she just didn't care.

"Okay, so I asked for a karaoke party for my twelfth birthday," Lynn started. Carrie felt her face beginning to grow warm. It wasn't fair that redheads blushed so much more easily than everyone else. "So my parents took me and some friends and Carrie to the Silver Dollar—you know, that diner where they have karaoke in the back room?" Theresa nodded. "Well, when we got there, we all told Carrie she had to sing because she has a great voice. Plus we thought it would be cute since she was only eight."

"Seven," Carrie corrected her. "I was seven."

"Okay, *seven*," Lynn said. "So anyway, she got up to do 'It's a Hard Knock Life.'"

Carrie felt the blush spread to her neck. She knew what was coming.

"She did a great job," Lynn continued. "She was like one of those kids on a TV talent show or something. She was dancing around the stage, singing her heart out. It was adorable. We used to have pictures, but Carrie made us throw most of them out. Because—" Lynn stopped, her green eyes sparkling.

Here it comes, Carrie thought, wishing she could disappear.

"Because, see, Carrie got *so* into the song that she didn't realize her skirt had gotten hitched up in the back. Every time she turned, the whole place could see her underwear!"

"Oh, my gosh!" Theresa said, grinning at Carrie.

"Tell them what kind of underwear it was," Stephanie reminded Lynn.

"Oh, that's right!" Lynn said. "I almost forgot. Carrie, you should tell them."

Carrie let out a sigh. Why not? She was already humiliated. "Scooby-Doo," she said. "It was Scooby-Doo underwear. And for *months* all my sister's friends called me Scooby."

Matt and Spence chuckled, and Theresa burst out laughing. "That is *such* a great story," she said between giggles. Then she slapped Carrie on the shoulder. "I can't believe you never told me that!"

"Must've slipped my mind," Carrie said sarcastically. She glared at her sister. "Thanks, Lynn."

"Oh, stop it," Lynn said, rolling her eyes. "You were only eight."

"*Seven*," Carrie insisted.

"All right—*seven*. It's not like it happened yesterday or anything."

"Yeah, don't be embarrassed, Carrie. It's

cute—really," Theresa said. "But," she added with a smirk, "just in case, maybe you should stay away from the Scooby underwear tomorrow—you know, for your audition?"

"You're trying out for the play?" Matt said.

"Well, I—"

"That's cool. Spence says he's gonna try out, too."

"Oh. Great," Carrie said, forcing a smile. She looked over at Theresa, who was still giggling about the whole Scooby story.

Wonderful, Carrie thought. Why had she thought that confiding in Theresa was a good idea? Thanks to her so-called *friend,* everyone was going to be expecting her to audition tomorrow. And with everyone expecting it, just how was she supposed to back out?

CHAPTER
Four

Carrie gave a nervous tug on the angel charm Anna had given her as she walked into Mrs. Wessex's classroom Tuesday morning. She looked around for Theresa and Anna, but they weren't there yet. Sharon was standing next to Matt's desk, though, so Carrie headed over there. "I'll have to talk to whoever's in charge of costumes," Sharon was saying to Matt, "to make sure they get mine right. I think Cindy should wear pants instead of a dress because, you know, it *is* supposed to be all modern or whatever. But they have to be the right kind of pants."

Carrie shook her head. The way Sharon was talking, it sounded like she'd already been given the lead role. Obviously, she just didn't consider any of the other fifth-grade girls serious competition—least of all Carrie.

"Hey, Carrie," Sharon said when she saw her. "We were just talking about the play. Do you think you'll end up working on costumes? Because I need to—"

"Yo, Matt, Scoob, what's up?"

Carrie turned and saw Spence coming over to them. Along with the backpack slung over one shoulder, he was carrying a skateboard covered with stickers from different bands.

"Scoob? What's that mean?" Sharon asked.

Carrie flushed. "It's nothing," she said.

Sharon frowned, then stood up straighter and grinned at Spence. "I'm Sharon Ross," she said. She gave her head a little shake so her blonde hair flipped behind her shoulder. "You must be the new guy."

Spence laughed. "Yeah, that's me," he said. "The true-blue newbie, kickin' it with Scooby." He dropped his backpack onto the chair next to Matt's and slid his skateboard under the desk. "But you can call me MC Spence."

"*O-kay*," Sharon said. She glanced at Matt, clearly uncertain what to make of his new friend. "MC Spence, huh?"

Spence nodded. "You got it."

"Are you . . . a *rapper*?"

"I'm working on it," Spence said. "I'm a fan

of the free verse, unrehearsed. It's like a rhymin' curse, for better or worse."

"Wow," Sharon gushed. "That is *so* cool. Did you just make that up—like, off the top of your head?"

Carrie tried not to laugh. So Spence read a lot of Dr. Seuss—what was the big deal? Sure, he seemed pretty good at the whole rhyming thing, but come on—Sharon looked like she was ready to ask for his autograph.

"Spence freestyles at the skate park sometimes," Matt said. "He's good."

"I bet," Sharon said. "I'll have to stop by and check it out sometime."

"You know it," Spence said. "The more the merrier. Hey—" he went on, turning to Carrie. "Did you end up getting that disk last night?"

Carrie nodded. "I've already listened to the whole thing twice," she said. "My favorite track is—"

"'Press Play'?"

"Yes! How did you know?"

"It's the best track on there," Spence said.

"We just got a new stereo system at home," Sharon announced. "You guys should come over so we can try it out."

"Nice," Spence said. "Carrie and I could bring the grooves—right, Scoob?"

Carrie winced. She'd thought she'd escaped that nickname four years ago, but now it looked like she was stuck with it all over again.

Just then Anna and Theresa came into the room, followed by Mrs. Wessex. Carrie walked over to them.

"Hey, is that Matt's friend?" Anna asked, pointing at Spence. "Theresa said you met him at the mall yesterday."

"Yeah, that's him," Carrie said. "MC Spence."

Anna raised her eyebrows. "Do people actually call him that?" she asked.

As if on cue, Sharon giggled and said, "Wow, MC Spence—you're *so* funny."

"Sharon does," Carrie replied. "How was the dentist?"

"No cavities," Anna said, baring her teeth.

"All right, class—let's get started," Mrs. Wessex said. Reluctantly, everyone shuffled to their seats. When they were finally settled, Mrs. Wessex held up a clipboard.

"I'm going to pass around this sign-up sheet for the class play. Now, this one is only for people who want to try out for a role. While it's going around, we'll talk about the other jobs that are available, and then I'll pass around a second clipboard so you can sign up for any committees that interest you. Maria, could you get this one going?" Mrs. Wessex asked.

Carrie watched as Maria took the clipboard and immediately scribbled her name at the top of the page. She passed it to Lauren Graham, who did the same. From there the clipboard continued down the row, and Carrie's eyes remained glued to it as it passed from one person to the next. It seemed like a lot of people were signing up.

"So, are you gonna do it?" Theresa whispered as she handed Carrie the clipboard.

Carrie lifted her shoulder in a half shrug, pretending not to care even though her heart was pounding like crazy. She stared down at the paper, gripping her pencil tightly. All she had to do was write two words—*Carrie Weingarten*.

She looked at the angel charm on her wrist and glanced toward Anna, hoping for encouragement. But Anna was writing in her notebook. Spence, on the other hand, who was just behind Anna and to the left, caught Carrie's eye. He nodded toward the clipboard and cocked his head.

Carrie pressed her lips together. *Come on, Carrie, just sign up!* she urged herself. If she didn't do something soon, other people were going to start noticing that she was just sitting there with the clipboard, too. But every time she told herself to just sign her name, it was like her hand didn't get the message.

She peeked over at Spence again to see if he was still watching, and he gave her an encouraging nod. *He thinks I should do it,* Carrie realized. And for a moment her spirits lifted. But then she realized that Spence didn't know her at all. He had no idea exactly what he was encouraging.

He hadn't witnessed her pathetic King Tut presentation. He didn't know that she blushed eighteen shades of red every time she walked into math class a little late. And he had no clue just how flustered she got speaking in front of people.

Of course, once he saw her audition, he'd know all of that. And he'd understand perfectly why she couldn't just sign her name and pass the clipboard on like everyone else. The problem was that this audition meant way too much to Carrie. The play wasn't just a fun school project for her. It was a chance to realize her dream. Or fail at it.

Carrie gazed down at the list one last time and clenched her pencil so hard, the tip of her index finger went white. Then, feeling her stomach turn, she handed the clipboard to Billy Rafuse. Without signing her name.

★   ★   ★

When lunchtime finally came, Carrie just wanted to be alone. She couldn't face having everyone ask why she hadn't signed up for the tryouts. So instead she retreated to her favorite spot—a beanbag chair in the back corner of the library.

There was only one thing that was going to make Carrie feel better right now, and that was writing. Thankfully, she always kept her journal nearby. She pulled her backpack onto her lap and began feeling around for the familiar spiral-bound book with its rough, glitter-encrusted cover.

That's strange, Carrie thought when she didn't find it immediately. It was usually right on top. She shifted the contents of her backpack around and even checked the front zippered pocket. No journal. Frustrated, Carrie fumbled through everything again but still had no luck.

Finally, she unzipped the backpack all the way and began removing items one at a time. Before long the backpack was empty and the floor in front of her was cluttered, but her journal was still nowhere in sight.

Carrie took a deep breath and retraced her steps. She knew she'd packed it that morning. She'd put it in just as her father had handed her a container of soy yogurt to go with the fried tempeh flat-bread sandwich he'd made her.

In fact, her journal had been the reason she'd double bagged the yogurt—to make sure it didn't leak and get the pages all sticky. Carrie looked at the stuff in front of her. Her notebook, her science book, a bunch of miscellaneous work sheets, her math book, three pens, a ruler, her lunch sack, and the yogurt, still double bagged. Where. Was. Her. Journal?

Could it have fallen out in one of the classrooms? Carrie shuddered at the idea, and her heart started pounding. If someone picked it up and read her private thoughts—especially all the stuff she'd written last night about how much she wanted to try out for the play but how scared she was to do it—she'd be mortified. Anyone who saw it would think she was a total baby. She could feel her face getting red just thinking about it.

Carrie peeked inside her empty backpack one last time, feeling around with her hand just to make sure. No luck—just bits of glitter. *Shoot,* Carrie thought. Now she was going to have to go back to all the classrooms she'd been in that morning and hope she could find the diary before someone else did.

CHAPTER
Five

Carrie let out a sigh as she jogged down a flight of stairs. So far she'd checked four of the five classrooms she'd been in that morning, two bathrooms, and most of the hallways. She'd asked every one of her teachers if they'd seen a journal with a blue sparkly cover, but none of them had.

Yet everywhere Carrie went, there seemed to be traces of blue glitter—on the floor here, under a chair there. It was like the journal had gotten up and run away all by itself. Or like Hansel and Gretel had stolen it and were leaving themselves a trail so they could find their way home.

Carrie shook her head, feeling like she was going crazy. She hated misplacing things.

She headed down the hall toward Mrs. Wessex's room. English had been her last class before lunch, and it was the only one she hadn't checked. She was almost there when she spotted something sparkling near the water fountain. She knelt down next to the fountain, shocked to see the corner of her journal peeking out.

"Thank goodness," she breathed. She grabbed the book and hugged it closely. The journal—and all of her private thoughts—were safe and sound, finally.

Carrie held the journal out in front of her, inspecting it. A lot of the glitter had come off, but that was okay. Everything else seemed to be in place. The blue satin bookmark was still hanging down the side, and—

"Oh, no. Where's Bob?" Carrie whispered. The end of the bookmark was frayed, and the silver unicorn charm that usually dangled from it was gone.

"Psst—over here," a voice called out.

Carrie blinked, then glanced around. She was the only one in the hallway.

"Who . . . who said that?" she whispered.

"Down here!" the squeaky voice called again. It seemed to be coming from . . . *under the fountain.*

Carrie bent down and stared at the carpet. There was a red pen cap lying there, but she didn't see anything else. She picked up the cap and examined it closely, wondering if maybe there was a tiny speaker hidden inside and someone was playing a joke on her.

"Ahem," the voice said. Carrie jumped. "Don't tell me you honestly think that piece of plastic is talking to you."

"I . . . uh . . ." Carrie swallowed nervously. She still couldn't tell where the voice was coming from.

"Then again, what would I expect from someone who would name a beautiful unicorn *'Bob'?*"

Carrie crouched down and peered under the fountain. *"Oh . . . my . . . gosh,"* she breathed.

There, backed against the wall, was a tiny, one-inch-tall white unicorn with a long, flowing mane, big brown eyes, and an iridescent horn.

"B-b-b-b-b-b-b?" was all Carrie could manage.

The unicorn nodded. "Bob," it said. "Nice name for a female unicorn. Remind me not to ask for your creative input when it comes to naming my children."

"B-b-b-b-b-b-b," Carrie stammered again.

"Yeah, I have a hard time saying it, too. Honestly. *Bob?* What were you thinking? Why couldn't you have given me a pretty name, like Francesca . . . or Cordelia—something with a little more personality? Or at the very least, something *slightly fem-i-nine.*"

"B-but . . . I—I didn't know you were a g-girl," Carrie whispered. She glanced left and right to make sure no one was witnessing her talking to what was probably just a figment of her imagination. "I—I named you after my uncle Bob. H-he was the one who gave me the bookmark. H-how did you—?"

"Come to life? Break free? Drag your journal under here?" Bob asked.

"Uh . . . yeah," Carrie murmured. She still couldn't believe what she was seeing—*and hearing.*

"Magic, a sharp horn, and determination," Bob said. "Now—do you think you could get me off this floor? Dust bunnies give me the willies. I swear I saw one over there with teeth."

Carrie put her journal down, looked around one more time, and held out her hand. The unicorn climbed on, her hooves softly padding against Carrie's palm. Carrie felt each hoof step. She saw the tiny creature right there in her hand. She had even heard it speak. But she still couldn't believe what was happening.

"I . . . I don't get it. I mean . . . what . . . how . . . *why* . . . ?"

"Long story," Bob replied, shaking her mane. "Let's just say some people on my side of the universe knew you needed a little encouragement, so they gave me permission to appear to you."

"Wait. *Your* side of the universe. Where's that? And *who* gave you permission? And how did they—?"

"Look, Carrie," Bob said, tapping her tiny hoof. "We could go back and forth about this forever and you still probably wouldn't understand it. Besides, like the cream in the middle of an Oreo and that gross stuff that you find in the corners of your eyes when you wake up in the morning, some things are best left unexamined. They just are what they are."

Carrie nodded uncertainly. "Okay . . . I guess." She reached down and gently petted the unicorn with the index finger of her free hand. Somehow the feeling of Bob's soft mane under her fingertip cemented things in Carrie's mind. "Wow, you actually *are* real."

"One hundred percent," Bob said. "No additives, no preservatives. Your dad would like that—not that he'd be able to talk to me. You're the only one who can see or hear me."

"Oh," Carrie said, taking a quick look down the hall. "So anyone who saw me right now—"

"Would think you were talking to your hand," Bob finished.

"Right," Carrie said. "Okay." She stood up

carefully, balancing Bob in her hand, and scanned the hallway again. Still alone. Thankfully. "Hey—what were you doing with my journal, anyway? Did you have to drag it around in order to get yourself loose?"

Bob cocked her head to one side. "Sure. We'll go with that."

"What do you mean?"

"I mean that's as good an explanation as any, so let's believe it."

Carrie scowled. "You can't just choose what to believe," she said. "It's either true or it isn't."

Bob shook her head. "Humans," she muttered, rolling her eyes. "I'd almost forgotten what an unenlightened species you are."

"Huh?"

"Forget it. We can talk about that later. Right now I need a comb and a mirror."

"Why?"

"So I can fix my hair," Bob said.

"Your *hair*?"

"Yes—my hair," Bob repeated. "You know—my mane and my tail? I like to keep myself looking presentable." Bob studied Carrie for a minute, then gave her a disappointed frown. "Not that I'd expect you to understand," she muttered.

"What did you say?"

"Nothing," Bob replied. "But you know, Lynn and Theresa are right—you really should put a little more effort into your appearance."

"What? How do you know Lynn and Theresa? And how do you know what they think of my appearance?"

"Well, I've been attached to your journal for the last year," Bob said, "and I'm a very good reader."

"You read my journal?!"

"Just skimmed it, really," Bob replied. "Unless there was something really juicy. But anyway, about that mirror—let's get going. I'm having a bad mane day."

"A bad mane day?"

Again Bob cocked her head at Carrie. "Of all people, I'd think *you'd* be able to relate," she said, eyeing Carrie's mass of red curls.

Carrie gasped. "That wasn't very nice."

"Hey—all I'm saying is that I think your hair and a barrette could be good friends."

"I thought you said you were sent here to encourage me," Carrie said. "Why are you being so insulting?"

"It's just friendly advice," Bob said. "Take it or leave it."

"I'll leave it, thanks."

"Fine," said Bob.

"Fine," echoed Carrie.

They were standing in the middle of the empty hallway, silent for a moment, until Bob said, *"About that mirror . . ."*

Carrie groaned. "Oh, all right. I suppose I could use a bathroom break before music class, anyway. Just let me put my journal in—hey!" Carrie picked up the journal and ran her hand along its glittery cover, fingering the spot where the silver clasp had been. "Bob—what happened to the lock? Did you break it off?"

Bob looked innocently at the ceiling. A little too innocently.

Carrie narrowed her eyes at the unicorn and noticed for the first time that the end of her horn was a bit bent—like she'd used it to pry something up.

"Bob," Carrie said suspiciously. She opened the journal and began flipping through it. As she did, a few small bits of paper fell loose from the spiral binding.

Carrie eyed the unicorn. "What did you do?" she asked, holding the little white animal close to her face. "Did you tear out some of the pages?"

Bob looked back at Carrie with twinkling eyes. *"May-be,"* she said.

"What did you do with them?"

Bob shook her head. "Sorry—can't say. But don't worry, I put them someplace where they'll do some good."

"Do some good? What are you—?"

Just then the bell rang, and Carrie jumped. Shoot. She had to get to class.

Carrie gazed at the unicorn. "I want those pages back, Bob—wherever you put them. But we'll have to talk about that later." Carrie stuffed her journal into her backpack, then looked from Bob to her bag and back again. "What should I do with you?" she asked.

"I suppose I can ride in the front pocket," Bob said, "but it's going to make these knots in my mane even worse. I'm going to need some detangler when we get home—and some moisturizer, too. The air in there is so dry."

"Fine," Carrie said. "Detangler and moisturizer. I'm sure my sister has plenty of both. Just get in. And get me those journal pages."

"You'll have them soon enough," Bob said with a smirk. Then she jumped into the backpack.

Carrie wanted to ask the unicorn what she

meant by "soon enough," but she had to get going if she didn't want to be late. Music class was on the other side of the school.

Thankfully she made it into Mrs. Hendrickson's room just as the final bell was ringing. There was only one seat left—the chair closest to the door—so Carrie sank into it, panting, and pulled her backpack onto her lap. When she'd recovered from her hundred-yard dash across the school, she glanced across the room and saw Anna and Theresa. They were both looking at her, concerned.

"Where were you during lunch?" Theresa mouthed, but Carrie just shook her head. She'd have to explain later—once she'd come up with a good explanation. Something other than, *I was just hanging out with my friend Bob the Unicorn.* That didn't seem like it would go over very well.

"Okay, it's time to get started," Mrs. Wessex said from the front of the room. "First we're going to hold the tryouts for the roles, and then we'll talk about what the rest of you will be doing for the play. For everyone who's auditioning, I'm going to give you a script and have you read in groups. Then Mrs. Hendrickson will have each of you sing for her."

Carrie looked down at her desk. Great. Now

she had to sit and watch her classmates try out for roles that she could have had a shot at if she hadn't been such a wimp. Oh, well. It wouldn't be so bad working on set design. She did like to draw. And at least she, Theresa, and Anna would be working together.

Mrs. Wessex slipped on her reading glasses and grabbed the audition sign-up sheet from the piano. She paused before reading the first name and cast a quick glance at some papers on the table behind her. When she turned back around, she stared right at Carrie.

"The first group will be . . . *Carrie Weingarten*— along with Sharon Ross and Kimberly Price." Mrs. Wessex smiled at Carrie as though they were sharing a secret joke, but all Carrie could do was stare.

She couldn't have heard that right. Had Mrs. Wessex really said her name? No way. Carrie hadn't written her name on that sign-up sheet. What was Mrs. Wessex thinking?

Sharon and Kimberly both walked up to the front of the room and took copies of scripts from their teacher, but Carrie was frozen in her seat.

"Carrie? Are you ready?" Mrs. Wessex prodded gently.

Carrie clutched her backpack closer, still not moving. "Ow!" she heard from inside the zippered pocket. Then there was a muffled, "Get up there!" Carrie glanced down to see the zipper coming undone and a tiny horn poking through the opening.

"Uh—" She gulped.

"Carrie?" Mrs. Wessex said again. "Why don't you come on up? I know you're really excited about this play."

You do? Carrie thought. *But how?* Then she saw it. The telltale blue glitter, sparkling in the light.

Bob had put the pages *someplace where they'd do some good,* she had said. So that's what she'd meant. Somehow she'd managed to get them to Mrs. Wessex. Carrie glared down at the unicorn.

"No need to thank me," Bob said. "Just go."

"Carrie?" Mrs. Wessex called.

Carrie looked at Anna and Theresa, who were both smiling and nodding at her.

"Bust a move, Scoob," Spence said, causing a few girls to giggle. His unique way of speaking—and the fact that he was Matt Dana's friend—had already earned him his share of admirers.

Carrie felt like dying, but what could she do? It was either sit there like an idiot while Mrs.

Wessex called her name again and again or get up and do the audition. Neither option appealed to her, but bowing out at this point seemed like an even worse idea.

So, with a deep breath, Carrie stood and walked up to the front of the room. Like it or not, she was about to try out for the class play.

CHAPTER
Six

Carrie could barely hold the script, her hands were shaking so badly. "I—I'm going to the prom, and you can't stop me," she read aloud. Her voice was trembling, too.

"Cindy, you know you're grounded this weekend," Sharon read as Cindy's stepmom. Sharon hadn't looked too happy when Mrs. Wessex had said Carrie would be reading the Cindy Rellar part, but then Mrs. Wessex had explained that she was simply listening to the way everyone read. She'd decide who should play which parts later.

"But I'm grounded *every* weekend," Carrie argued as Cindy. She looked at Sharon and tried to imagine her as a cruel stepmom who would never let Carrie do anything. It wasn't much of a stretch. "You always let *her* go anywhere she wants," Carrie continued, pointing at Kimberly, who was reading the part of Cindy's stepsister, Staci. "I did all my chores, just like you asked. You can't keep me from going to the dance!"

"Get real, Cindy," Kimberly read, sticking her nose in the air. She, too, seemed pretty well suited for the role she was reading. "If Mom let you go to the dance, what would you wear, anyway? Those *jeans* you have on every day? And that ratty old sweatshirt?"

"I could borrow one of your dresses," Carrie shot back. "You have plenty." Her voice had more of an edge to it now—probably because she was beginning to feel a little angry on her character's behalf. Cindy's stepsister and stepmother were so nasty.

As they went on, Carrie continued to feel less like she was reading a part and more like she, Sharon, and Kimberly were having an actual fight. By the end of the scene she'd all but forgotten that the entire class was watching—until Mrs. Wessex cut in.

"Nice job," Mrs. Wessex said after Sharon had read the last line. "Great work, all of you."

Carrie blinked. She'd been so focused on the scene, she'd almost forgotten where she was.

"Now let's hear each of you sing something,"

Mrs. Wessex continued, "and then we'll move on to the next group. Carrie, why don't you go first?"

"Oh. Uh, okay," Carrie said.

"We're simply going to have everyone sing two verses of 'The Happy Wanderer,' which Mrs. Hendrickson tells me you've been working on in class. Mrs. Hendrickson will do a brief introduction on the piano so you can get the key, and then you can come in. Ready, Carrie?"

Carrie nodded, but she felt her stomach tossing and turning all over again. Reading was one thing—singing was on a completely different level. There was much more potential for embarrassment.

As Mrs. Hendrickson began, Carrie's mouth suddenly went dry. She licked her lips, but it didn't seem to do the trick. When the music came around to the spot where Carrie was supposed to come in, she opened her mouth, but no words came out—just a little squeak.

A few students chuckled, and Carrie coughed and cleared her throat.

"Would you like me to start again?" Mrs. Hendrickson asked, giving her a warm smile.

"Yes, please," Carrie said, her voice barely a whisper. She cleared her throat again and moistened her lips.

Sharon let out a sigh. "I guess we'll be here for a while," she muttered.

Carrie tried to ignore her. She knew Sharon was just mad that she hadn't gotten to read Cindy's lines.

But as Mrs. Hendrickson started playing the song a second time, Carrie felt her mouth going dry again, and she worried that Sharon might be right. Then, just before Mrs. Hendrickson reached Carrie's cue, Carrie felt a prick right above her ankle. She glanced down and saw Bob perched on her shoe. She was so shocked, she gasped slightly. It wasn't much of a noise, but it was enough that when Mrs. Hendrickson finished the intro, this time Carrie was able to find her voice.

She blurted out the first few words, realizing the notes were a little off, but at least she'd managed to get started. And by the second line Carrie had the melody under control. Eventually, she was able to concentrate on the music and shut out everything else—even Bob.

"My backpack on my baaaaack," she finished. Then she waited with her eyes closed as Mrs. Hendrickson played the last notes on the piano.

The room was absolutely silent, and Carrie

swallowed a few times, afraid to make eye contact with anyone. Then, to her surprise, people began clapping. Carrie opened her eyes to see Anna and Theresa with their thumbs up, grinning wildly. Then she saw Maria Mancini mouth, "Wow," to Lauren Graham, and Lauren nodded. Amazingly, no one seemed to be laughing.

"Carrie, that was beautiful," Mrs. Hendrickson said.

Carrie slowly met her gaze. "Really?" she asked, her heart thumping in her chest.

"Yes," Mrs. Wessex agreed. "What a wonderful voice you have! I'm so glad you decided to audition," she added, her eyes twinkling. She reached for the journal pages on the table and passed them to Carrie with a smile.

Carrie felt a few light pokes at her ankle and looked down to see Bob prancing back and forth between her shoes, doing some kind of weird unicorn victory dance.

Okay, so maybe Bob had done her a favor after all. Now that the audition was over, Carrie was glad she'd gone through with it. It hadn't been nearly as bad as she'd expected. And Mrs. Wessex and Mrs. Hendrickson—and even some of the other kids—seemed to think she'd actually done okay.

Maybe she had a shot at making her dream come true after all.

"Fifty-one, fifty-two, sixty-three, sixty-four—"

"Hey! You skipped ahead," Bob interrupted.

Carrie paused, holding the toothbrush in midair. "Okay. You know that whole *one hundred strokes a day* thing is just a myth, right?" she said. "It's not really going to make your hair any shinier."

"Interesting theory," Bob said. "I'll think about it while you do the last forty-six strokes."

Carrie rolled her eyes, but she went on brushing. It was easier than listening to the demanding little unicorn whine about how matted her mane was getting from traveling by backpack.

To pacify her, Carrie had gotten a spare toothbrush from the school nurse after lunch and promised to comb out Bob's hair during social studies. Mrs. Wessex was always good about giving out bathroom passes.

"Ninety-nine, one hundred," Carrie finished. "There—are you satisfied?"

Bob pranced back and forth on the countertop, tossing her freshly brushed mane like a show horse. "Ahhh," she sighed. "Much better, don't you think?"

Carrie rolled her eyes. "Whatever you say, Bob."

"*Bob!*" the unicorn scoffed. "Ugh. You have got to stop calling me that."

"What do you want me to call you?"

"Anything," Bob said. "Anything. But. Bob."

"Jim?" Carrie ventured with a smirk.

"Oh, you're a riot," Bob said.

"Sorry," Carrie replied with a chuckle. "How about . . ." She racked her brain for a name the unicorn would like. "Sabrina?"

Bob shook her mane. "Sounds like a cat," she said.

"All right. What about . . . Ella?"

"As in *Ella-phant*?" Bob snorted. "No thanks."

"Wow, you're picky," Carrie said.

"No, I'm not," Bob replied. "You just haven't mentioned any good names yet."

"*O-kay* . . . Mary?"

"Too plain."

"Angelica?"

"Sounds snobby."

"Margaret?"

"Too stiff."

"Polly?"

"As in *'wants a cracker'*?"

"Bob!" Carrie snapped. "Those are all perfectly good names."

"This from the girl who named me *Bob*," Bob muttered.

Carrie shook her head. "Forget it. We'll have to come up with something later. Right now we have to get back to class."

"Okay," Bob said, checking herself out in the mirror one more time. "But first let's go look at that cast list."

"The cast list?"

"Yeah. Didn't Mrs. Hendrickson say she'd have it posted by the end of the day?"

"Well, yeah, but—"

"It's the end of the day. So let's go look," Bob said.

Carrie groaned. "I don't know."

"What do you mean, you don't know? Don't you want to see what part you got?"

"But what if I didn't get one?"

"Are you kidding? Of course you got one. Your audition was great. Didn't you hear your teachers and your friends? They were all gushing about your voice."

"Yeah," Carrie said, "but they're my teachers and my friends. What else are they going to say?"

Bob stamped her hooves impatiently on the sink. "You're a piece of work, you know it? You have to believe in yourself, Carrie."

"I do," Carrie insisted. "Most of the time."

"Yeah, well . . . no time like the present," Bob said.

"What's that supposed to—wait! Bob!" Carrie called, but it was too late. Bob had speared Carrie's bathroom pass with her crooked horn and scooted under the door. By the time Carrie had thrown the toothbrush into her backpack and gotten out of the bathroom, Bob was rounding the corner at the end of the hall.

"Bob!" Carrie hissed, but the little unicorn continued at a gallop, and Carrie had no choice but to chase her. She raced after Bob down one hall and around the corner, then down another hall and up a flight of stairs.

She finally caught up to Bob just outside Mrs. Hendrickson's classroom, arriving there out of breath for the second time that day. Bob slowed to a trot and then pranced around the group of kids who were crowded around the music room door. Carrie stood back, noticing that most of her class was out there.

"What's going on?" Carrie said to no one in particular.

"Mrs. Wessex let us out early to look at the cast list," Maria replied. "You should check it out," she added with a grin.

Carrie looked at the group of people clustered there. They were all scanning a piece of paper that was taped to the outside. The cast list.

I can't do it, Carrie thought. *I can't look.*

Just then Anna, who was near the front of the group with Theresa, caught sight of her. "Hey, Carrie! Come see where your name is!" she called.

"I—I got a part?" Carrie murmured.

"You've got to be joking, girl," Spence said, clapping her on the back. "With that voice you really think there's a chance you *didn't* get one?"

"Well . . ."

"Carrie! Come look!" Theresa called.

Oh, boy, Carrie thought. *Here goes.* Slowly, she walked forward. Her friends seemed excited— that was a good sign, right? Then again, they hadn't expected Carrie to try out for the play in the first place. They'd probably be psyched to see her name next to *Prom Guest #1.* Carrie, on the other hand, was hoping for more, and she was afraid she was about to be disappointed.

"Believe in yourself!" she heard a little voice call. Then she heard the sound of tiny hooves prancing away down the hall.

All right, Carrie thought. *Here goes.*

She walked to the front of the crowd and scanned the names on the list. Kimberly had gotten the part of Cindy's stepmom, and Lauren Graham was Staci, Cindy's stepsister. Maria was playing the other stepsister, Drew, and Jeremy and Billy were part of the prom band.

Carrie continued to run through the list, all the way down to the tiniest parts—but she didn't see her name anywhere. Her stomach tightened as a wave of disappointment rushed over her. It didn't seem fair. She'd actually had the guts to try out—well, with a little push from Bob, but still. And look what had happened.

She hadn't even managed to get Princess Charming, who only had a couple of lines and then sang one song with the chorus. And forget about Prom Guest #1—that had gone to Sally Betze.

"So—what do you think it means?" Theresa asked.

That I suck, Carrie thought. Why were her friends being so mean, anyway? Were they trying to make a point by showing her that she hadn't made the list?

"You should go in now," Anna said. "Mrs. Hendrickson is in there."

Carrie squinted. "What are you talking about?" she asked.

Theresa rolled her eyes. "Didn't you see?" she said, tapping the top of the paper. There were a few sentences there, but Carrie had skipped over them and gone straight to the list of names. Now, however, she took a minute to read them.

> *The lead role of Cindy Rellar is being adapted. Sharon Ross and Carrie Weingarten, please come see me ASAP.*
> —Mrs. Hendrickson

Carrie's eyes widened. *Adapted?* What did that mean?

"Excuse me, I need to see the list," Sharon said, pushing her way through the crowd.

"Hey, Sharon, there's a—" Theresa began.

"Hold on," Sharon said, waving her hand impatiently. "I have to find my name." She scanned the list, just as Carrie had, and then blinked.

"I don't get it," she said. "Why isn't my name up there? Hey, wait a second . . . I don't even see Cindy Rellar listed. What's going on?"

"That's what I was trying to tell you," Theresa said. She pointed at the note.

Sharon read it, and her expression settled into a deep frown. "*Adapted?* What does that mean? And why would she want to talk to both of us?" she added, scowling at Carrie.

"I don't know," Carrie said.

"Well, let's go find out," Sharon replied. Without hesitation, she pushed open the music room door and marched in.

"You wanted to see us?" Sharon said as she and Carrie approached the piano, where Mrs. Hendrickson was looking over some music.

"Yes," Mrs. Hendrickson said, standing. "I wanted to talk to you about the lead role— Cindy Rellar. You see, Mrs. Wessex and I were troubled over what to do. We had two extremely talented young ladies and only one lead role. It just didn't seem right to choose either one of you when you were both so good."

Carrie's jaw dropped. Mrs. Hendrickson was talking about her. *She* was one of the extremely talented young ladies.

"So . . . what are you saying?" Sharon asked. Her whole face had gone white. "Neither one of us gets to be in the play?"

Mrs. Hendrickson laughed. "No, of course not," she said. "What we decided to do is split the lead role into *two* lead roles, which would have been hard to explain on the cast list. Carrie will be Cindy, and you, Sharon, will be Cindy's best friend—Rae Punzille, who's staying with Cindy and Cindy's family while her mother is away on business."

"I'm playing . . . ?" Carrie couldn't even say it.

"Cindy Rellar—yes," Mrs. Hendrickson said. "Is that all right?"

"Oh—*yeah*. I mean—yes—definitely," Carrie stammered.

The lead. Carrie had actually won *the lead* in the class play! Sure, she was splitting it with Sharon, but that didn't matter. It was still the lead role—exactly what she had wanted but had been too scared to really hope for. She couldn't wait to tell Anna and Theresa.

"We're going to divide up the lines that were originally Cindy's between the two of you," Mrs. Hendrickson explained, "and Mrs. Wessex will add a little more dialogue for both of you so you'll still have plenty to do. Then we'll have you sing a duet with two solo parts. You have such nice voices—I can't wait to hear how beautiful you sound together!"

The lead role. A duet. Two solo parts. Two. Solo. Parts. *Wait a second* . . . solo? The word bounced around in Carrie's brain like a Super Ball let loose in a gymnasium. Suddenly everything began to sink in. Carrie was going to be acting in front of a whole audience. And singing. Solo. *Alone.* She gulped.

"Mrs. Wessex will have the new scripts for

you tomorrow," Mrs. Hendrickson said. "We worked on them a bit this afternoon, and she's making the finishing touches at home tonight so they'll be all ready for our first rehearsal. Congratulations, both of you."

"Thanks, Mrs. Hendrickson," Sharon said.

"Yeah, thanks," Carrie echoed, but her mouth had gone dry again and her voice was a bit raspy.

"So—what did she say?" Theresa asked as Carrie and Sharon exited the music room.

"They're splitting the lead," Sharon said. "Carrie's playing Cindy, and they're writing an entirely new role for me."

"Way to go, Scoob!" Spence said.

"That's awesome!" Theresa added.

"Wow, Carrie," Anna said. "You got the lead!"

"Actually," Sharon cut in, "*I* got the lead. I'm playing Rae Punzille. Mrs. Wessex is creating the role just for me."

"If Rae Punzille is the lead, how come the play is called *Cindy Rellar: A Modern Fairy Tale*?" Anna asked.

"I don't know," Sharon replied, tossing her hair over her shoulder. "All I know is that Mrs. Hendrickson and Mrs. Wessex thought I deserved a bigger part, so they're making one for me. I'd call that the lead. And I wouldn't be surprised if they changed the name of the play, either."

"*O-kay,*" Theresa said. She raised her eyebrows at Carrie and Anna.

"Hey—keep it chill, ladies," Spence cut in. "It's all good. The important thing is that you both got parts. And even more important is the fact that I'm going to be the emcee."

"The *emcee?*" Theresa questioned.

"Spence is the narrator," Matt said, stepping forward. He'd been so quiet, Carrie hadn't even noticed him standing there before.

"You say narrator, I say emcee," said Spence. "It's all the same. But what about you, dude? You're the man—you're Charlie Prinze."

Carrie glanced back at the list. Matt was playing the male lead? How had she missed that?

"That's awesome, Matt," Theresa said.

"Yeah," said Matt, but he didn't exactly look thrilled.

"Mrs. Wessex *made* Matt audition," Anna explained. "She said there weren't enough boys on the list and that he was a really good reader, so . . ."

Matt scowled. "So I'm Charlie Prinze— Cindy's prom date."

"Cheer up, buddy," Spence said, clapping

him on the shoulder. "Maybe you can pick Carrie up for the prom on your skateboard."

Matt's frown dissolved, and he raised his eyebrows. "Do you think Mrs. W. would go for that?" he asked.

"Why not?" said Spence. "It's supposed to be a modern fairy tale. Tell you what—we'll start working on getting your skateboard in the play just as soon as I convince her to change *narrator* to *emcee* in the program."

Matt chuckled. "Cool," he said.

"Well," Sharon said, folding her arms across her chest, "for all we know, you might be taking Rae to the prom now—not Cindy. We'll just have to wait and see when Mrs. Wessex hands out the new scripts tomorrow."

Carrie swallowed hard. Sharon seemed pretty upset about the way things had turned out.

"Hey, um . . . congratulations, Sharon," she said, trying to smooth things over. "I'm really glad we're going to be in the play together. And I know I'll feel a lot more comfortable being onstage with you. It's just like you said at lunch yesterday, remember? You'll be up there to help me out if I get nervous." She gave Sharon a weak smile, hoping she would agree that things really had turned out for the best.

Sharon held Carrie's gaze, but she didn't return the smile. "Yeah, I guess so," she said. "But you know, even I'm not going to be able to help you if you just freeze up the way you did in your audition today. If you don't kick that stage fright before opening night, you're going to ruin the whole play. Come on, Kimberly. Let's go," she added, and the two of them headed off down the hallway.

Carrie stared after Sharon, realizing that even though she'd gotten through the audition okay, her troubles weren't over. Now she had an entirely new problem to confront: her costar.

CHAPTER
Seven

"Can you even *see* with all that hair in your eyes?" Bob asked.

It was Wednesday afternoon, and Carrie had stopped at the bathroom before play rehearsal to give Bob her daily brushing.

"Of course I can," Carrie said. Although she did have to kind of squint to look past her bangs sometimes. "Ninety-eight, ninety-nine, one hundred," she counted. "There." She stuffed the toothbrush into her backpack and watched as Bob pranced back and forth on the counter, admiring her mane.

"You know what I don't get?" Carrie asked.

"What?"

"Why you care so much about how you look when I'm the only one who can see you," Carrie said. "Are all unicorns this vain?"

Bob stopped and faced Carrie. "It's not vanity,"

she insisted, stamping her hooves. "I just take good care of myself, and I happen to take a certain pride in my appearance. Unlike you, I'm not scared to stand out."

Carrie scrunched her eyebrows together. "*What* are you talking about?"

"You," Bob said, "and the way you hide behind that wall of hair. It's like you're afraid to be noticed."

Carrie clicked her tongue. "I am not," she said. "I just don't care all that much about my appearance."

"You *say* that," Bob said. "But I'm not so sure it's true."

"Of course it's true," Carrie said. "If I cared about my appearance, I'd let Theresa find me some hair clips and get some lip gloss and try to look like the cover of every teen magazine in the grocery store."

"*Maybe,*" Bob admitted. "But if what you say is true and you really *don't* care about your appearance, why did you get so worked up about trying out for the play?"

"Because I was afraid I'd make a fool of myself," Carrie said.

"You mean by messing up lines or singing off-key or something and then having people laugh at you or think you're stupid because of the way you would *appear* to them?"

"Well . . . *yeah*, but—"

"See, I think it's pretty much the same. It all comes down to worrying about the way other people see you," Bob said. "Which is why you don't even want to let anybody look."

"What do you mean?"

"I mean," Bob said slowly, "that you let your hair hang in your face so you can hide. When you don't want people to know what you're thinking or how you feel, you just look down, and that mass of curls covers everything—your eyes, your expression—everything."

"You're crazy," Carrie said.

"You're the one talking to a unicorn," Bob reminded her.

"True," Carrie replied, "and if I don't stop, I'm going to be late for rehearsal." She hefted her backpack onto the counter and unzipped the front pocket. "Hop in."

"Fine," Bob said. "But when you're reading your lines today, get that hair out of your face and speak up. Don't be afraid to really try."

Carrie pushed open the bathroom door and stepped into the hallway. "You sound like my mother," she told the unicorn.

"Who does?" Sharon asked.

Carrie started, surprised to see Sharon just one step behind her. "Oh, um . . . no one. I was just practicing. For the play. Trying to, you know, figure out how I would feel if I were Cindy."

Sharon rolled her eyes. "It's called *getting into character*," she said. "We've worked on that a lot in my drama class."

"Oh," Carrie replied. She was already sick of hearing about Sharon's drama class. Fortunately, Sharon was silent as they walked down the hall. Unfortunately, it was the kind of silence that made Carrie feel like Sharon wanted to bite her head off, chew it up, and spit it out.

When they were almost to the music room, Sharon stopped and turned to Carrie. "Look," she said, "I'm not exactly thrilled about the whole double-lead thing."

"Really?" Carrie said. "Gee—I never would have guessed."

"Funny," Sharon sneered. "Anyway, the thing is, I want this play to be good."

"So do I," Carrie said.

"Well, that means *you* need to be good. You're going to be onstage for most of the play, so you can't freeze or forget your lines or stutter through them."

Carrie swallowed hard. Those were all things she was afraid she might do. They were all things she *had* done when she was giving her King Tut presentation, and that had only had to be two minutes long. The play would probably last at least an hour, and like Sharon said— Carrie was going to be onstage for most of it. "I—I know," she told Sharon.

"Good," Sharon said. "So here's what you need to do. Today is just a read through."

"A read through?"

"Yeah. That's when the cast just sits in a circle and reads straight through the script so that everyone gets to do all their lines."

"Oh," Carrie said. That didn't sound too bad.

"But even though it's just a read through, there are two things you should start working on now: your voice and your movements."

Carrie tilted her head. Why was Sharon telling her all of this? She actually seemed to be helping.

"When you're onstage," Sharon continued, "you have to realize that it's not like TV."

"Thank goodness," Carrie muttered. She was scared enough about performing in front of an auditorium full of people. She certainly didn't need the added pressure of being broadcast to millions more.

"On TV, actors have microphones and sound people to make their voices loud enough. Plus they have cameras to do close-ups so you can always see if they're smiling or upset or whatever. But onstage, it's just *you*."

Again Carrie swallowed hard. If this was supposed to be a pep talk, it wasn't working.

"So when you're reading your lines, remember these two things: you need to talk really loud and make your movements really big. Got it?"

Carrie squinted, then nodded. "I guess," she said.

"And you need to start doing both of those today," Sharon went on.

"But I thought you said it's just a . . . *read through*?" Carrie asked.

"It is," Sharon said. "But if you start out reading in your regular voice and not moving around at all, you're going to get used to it. Then when we start practicing for real, you'll have to break those habits. And considering the fact that you already have stage fright to worry about . . ."

Carrie sucked in her breath and rubbed her sweaty palms together. The butterflies in her stomach made her wonder if it was possible to have stage fright when she wasn't even onstage.

And if she got it right now, would it be called *hall fright*? Or just *Sharon fright*?

"I could give you a few other tips," Sharon offered.

"You have . . . *more*?" Carrie asked, her eyes widening.

Sharon must have noticed the concern in Carrie's eyes because she backed off. "Actually, why don't you just work on those for today: talking loud—it's called projecting," she added, "and making your movements big. Use your hands, your arms, your head—you could even stand up, although Mrs. Wessex will probably want us all to just sit at the table today."

Carrie nodded. "All right," she said, taking a deep breath. "Talk loud, use big movements. I can do that."

"That's it," Sharon said. "And if you do it from the beginning, it'll be easy when you're finally onstage."

"Right," Carrie said.

Sharon started toward the music room again, but Carrie stopped her.

"Um, Sharon?" she said. "Thanks."

Sharon just shrugged. "Like I said—I want this play to be good."

Carrie nodded and followed her into their first

rehearsal, feeling a little guilty for having assumed that Sharon would be hard to work with.

When they got inside, Carrie noticed that the room was set up exactly as Sharon had predicted. There was a big table in the center of the room, with chairs around it, and there was a script at each seat. Matt and Spence were already there, along with Maria, Lauren, Kimberly, Sally, Jeremy, Billy, and the rest of the cast. It looked like Sharon and Carrie were the last to arrive.

"Okay, everyone—we're all here now," Mrs. Wessex said. "Let's get started." Everyone filed over to the table and took a seat. Carrie ended up between Maria and Lauren with Sharon, Matt, and Spence directly across from her.

"We're just doing a read through today," Mrs. Wessex said. Carrie caught Sharon's eye and smiled. She'd been right about everything so far. Again Sharon just shrugged like it was old news to her—like she'd been going to play rehearsals every day of her life.

"If everyone will flip to page one, we'll jump right in," Mrs. Wessex said. The noise of rustling paper filled the room as everyone opened their scripts. "As you can see, the play now starts with a solo by Cindy."

Carrie's shoulders tensed. She had to start the whole play? *Alone?*

"But we'll be skipping the songs for today and focusing on the straight speaking parts."

Phew, Carrie thought. She needed more time to work up to the whole solo idea. "So that means we'll be starting with you, Ward," Mrs. Wessex said, nodding to Spence. He'd already given her his whole MC Spence spiel, but Mrs. Wessex was a stickler for using people's real names.

"That's cool," Spence said. He cleared his throat and began to read. "Good evening, ladies and gentlemen. Welcome to the fifth-grade production of *Cindy Rellar: A Modern Fairy Tale.* Our story unfolds—" Spence set down his script and looked up. "Hey, Mrs. W.—I thought this was supposed to be modern."

"It is, Ward."

"So then why am I saying stuff like, 'our story unfolds'? Shouldn't it be more, I don't know . . . hip?"

Mrs. Wessex furrowed her brow. "What did you have in mind?"

Spence shrugged. "I don't know, something like . . . *Yo! This is the story of Cindy Rellar / Wants to go to the prom, but they keep her in the cellar. / She's got a harsh stepmom and some stepsisters, too; /*

They're in her face, they're on her case, they want her glass shoe. / She—"

"Uh, thank you, Ward," Mrs. Wessex interrupted amidst the giggles and squeals of everyone around the table. Matt was nearly doubled over with laughter, and Sharon was staring at Spence with awe. Even Carrie, who was trying so hard to focus on the tips Sharon had given her, had to smile.

"I'll definitely take that into consideration," Mrs. Wessex said. "But for now, why don't we just read what's in the script?"

"Whatever you say, Mrs. W.," Spence said. And he went back to reading his regular lines, which, admittedly, sounded kind of boring after the little rap he'd just done.

When Spence was finished with the introduction, Mrs. Wessex spoke up again. "Well, maybe we *could* spice that up a bit," she said, giving Spence a little smile. "But let's keep going for now. Carrie?"

Carrie checked the script. The next lines were hers. She cleared her throat and took a deep breath, then glanced across the table at Sharon.

"Big," Sharon mouthed. *"And loud."* Carrie nodded, and Sharon gave her a thumbs-up. Then Carrie cleared her throat one more time and got ready.

According to the stage directions in the script, Cindy was supposed to be cleaning the floor as the play started. *Big movements,* Carrie thought as she set her script on the table. *And talk loud.* She sat up straight and gripped an imaginary sponge in one hand and pretended to be carrying a bucket in the other. "Work, work, work!" she bellowed. "That's all I ever do around here! If only my stepsisters—"

"Uh, Carrie?" Mrs. Wessex cut in. "I'm glad you've found your voice, but it probably doesn't need to be quite that loud."

Carrie blinked at Sharon, who seemed to be smirking. "I was just trying to, um . . . *project,*" Carrie said, hoping she'd used the right word.

"Oh, yes." Mrs. Wessex nodded. "I understand. And that's very important. But this is just a read through, and there will be microphones hanging above the stage."

"There will?" Carrie shot a fierce look at Sharon, who just shrugged innocently.

"Of course," Mrs. Wessex said. "So I'm sure your voice will carry beautifully."

"Oh," Carrie said. "Right."

"So, why don't we start that scene again, and just use your normal speaking voice. That should be fine."

Carrie looked back to the script, trying to focus on her lines, but she couldn't help feeling a little stupid. Of course, it didn't help that Maria and Lauren both had their hands over their mouths like they were trying hard not to laugh.

Forget them, Carrie told herself. *Just read.* She cleared her throat a third time and pretended to be holding her sponge and bucket again. "Work, work, work," she repeated, this time in her regular voice. "That's all I ever do around here. If only my stepsisters would help out. Then maybe I'd have time to go to the mall and find a dress for the prom."

At that point the stage directions called for Cindy to continue cleaning the floor while the narrator said a few more lines. So Carrie dipped her imaginary sponge in her imaginary bucket and pretended to scrub the table.

Big movements, she told herself, moving her hand in a large circle. Unfortunately, her big movement knocked over Lauren's big water bottle and made a big puddle in the middle of the table.

"Carrie!" Lauren yelled.

"I didn't mean to," Carrie said. "I was just . . . pretending to scrub the floor."

Mrs. Wessex took a deep breath. "Matt, could

you go get us some paper towels, please? Charlie Prinze doesn't come in until the next scene."

"Sure," Matt said, standing and sprinting toward the door.

"Walk, please!" Mrs. Wessex called after him. Matt slowed down until he got to the door, but everyone heard his footsteps speed up again as soon as he was in the hall.

Mrs. Wessex sighed and shook her head. "All right, let's keep going," she said. "But why don't we just focus on *reading* today," she added, looking straight at Carrie. "This is a small space, and we don't want to have any more accidents. There will be plenty of time to work out all of our movements and gestures when we begin practicing on the stage."

"Yeah, no more scrubbing the table, Carrie," Sharon joked. "At least not till Matt gets back with the paper towels."

Everyone else laughed, but Carrie just bit her lip. She felt like such an idiot. Partly for yelling her lines and knocking over Lauren's water, but mostly for having believed that Sharon would actually try to help her.

"All right, calm down, everyone," Mrs. Wessex said, looking a bit weary. "Ward, let's take it from your next line. Ready?"

"No worries, Mrs. W.—I've got it all under control," Spence said. "Check this out." Spence stood up, holding a piece of paper on which he'd scribbled some words instead of his script. Then he started rapping again.

"The big dance was only a week away,

But Cindy Rellar didn't have no time to play.

She had to cook, she had to clean, she had to scrub the floor,

And whenever she finished, they just gave her more—

More work to do, more jobs, more stress,

When all Cindy wanted was to score a dress."

Spence finished his rap and glanced up. "What do you think?" he asked. Everyone around the table started clapping and whistling, but Mrs. Wessex was holding her head in her hands.

"It was . . . *very imaginative*, Ward," she said when the applause had died down. "But we can't just have everyone changing their lines around anytime they wish. I think it's important at this point that we stick to the script."

Spence frowned. "But—"

Just then Matt returned . . . riding his skateboard. He rolled across the music room floor, tossed a bundle of paper towels to Spence, and then came to a dramatic stop right in front of

Mrs. Wessex, kicking his board into the air and catching it.

"Matthew Dana!" Mrs. Wessex exclaimed. "What do you think you're doing? You know you can't ride that thing in here!"

"It's for the play," Matt said.

Mrs. Wessex's eyebrows shot into the air. "It's . . . *what*?"

"For the play," Matt repeated. "See, Spence and I figured Charlie Prinze would be a skater. Hey—do you think Mrs. Hendrickson would let me use the risers as rails?"

Mrs. Wessex glanced around the table, then pressed her eyes closed. "Let's take five, everybody," she said. "Use the bathroom, get a drink of water. I'll wipe off the table, and we'll meet right back here."

Nobody needed to hear that announcement twice. In no time they were all on their feet and headed out of the room. But just as Carrie was about to go, Mrs. Wessex stopped her.

"Carrie," she said, "as one of the leads in the play, I think you could help to set a more serious tone for these rehearsals. Now, I know you're nervous, but when you come back from the break, I'd like you to try to focus on simply reading your lines. No shouting, no actions, no gestures—just straightforward reading. Do you think you can do that?"

"Um, sure," Carrie said. "I'll try."

"Thank you," Mrs. Wessex said. "I think that will make a big difference."

Carrie's heart sank as she walked out the door. So far, the rehearsal wasn't going very well, and it seemed like Mrs. Wessex thought Carrie was to blame. She'd been so stupid to trust Sharon.

Almost as stupid as Mrs. Wessex was to trust me with a lead role, Carrie thought.

CHAPTER
Eight

"I hate that store, you know," Carrie whispered as she walked out of Sara's with Bob perched on her shoulder. "And I don't see how you're going to make that big green butterfly clip work in your mane."

"Trust me," the tiny unicorn said. "It'll be perfect. You'll see."

"Whatever," Carrie muttered. She was just glad to be out of there and on her way to Sound Factory. According to Spence, they had some new V-3 disks that were "kickin'," as Spence said. Carrie wanted to grab a copy before they sold out.

That was where she'd been headed when Bob had spotted Sara's and thrown a uni-tantrum, demanding that Carrie stop and buy her a few things at the accessory store—a ring she could wear as an anklet, a pair of hoop earrings to use as chokers, a temporary rose tattoo for her left flank, and the green butterfly hair clip, which Carrie thought would look even more ridiculous on Bob than it would on her.

"Okay," Bob said as Carrie headed for the music store. "We have fifteen minutes before we have to meet your friends, right?"

"Right," Carrie replied. She had agreed to meet up with Anna and Theresa after rehearsal to help them scout out prop and costume ideas for the play.

"So . . . whaddya say we make a quick stop in the bathroom so I can try on some of my new stuff?"

"No way," Carrie said. "I'm going to Sound Factory."

"Pleeeeease," said Bob.

"Look—you're lucky I even bought you that stuff after what you got me into," Carrie snapped. An older couple walking past stared at Carrie with concern, and Carrie realized she needed to be more careful about talking to Bob in public.

"You should be excited about the play," Bob said from her perch on Carrie's shoulder. "You got a lead role. That's what you wanted, right?"

"Yeah, back when I was stupid enough to think I could actually pull it off. Weren't you listening at rehearsal today?"

Bob was quiet for a second. "Actually, I took a nap," she admitted. "I need to get my—"

"Beauty sleep?" Carrie guessed. Bob nodded. "Oh, but you're not vain at all," Carrie said sarcastically.

"All right, so I'm a little vain," Bob said. "At least I dare to be myself."

Carrie groaned. "Not this again."

"Sorry," said Bob, "but you're going to keep hearing it till you get it. You need to stop worrying so much about what everyone else thinks and just do your best. And get that hair out of your eyes," she added.

Carrie shook her head. "Vain," she said.

"Stubborn," Bob shot back.

"Sound Factory," Carrie said, "finally." And she headed into the store.

"Ugh," Bob said. "I'm going to take another nap. Wake me up if you see a mirror." And with that, she leaped off Carrie's shoulder and dove straight into the Sara's bag.

"Good riddance," Carrie muttered. She walked over to the hip-hop section and went straight to the *V*s. There wasn't much in there, and it didn't take her long to reach the end. "Shoot," she said. "They're sold out."

"I could burn you a copy," a voice said.

Carrie glanced up to see Spence flipping through the new releases. "Really?" she asked.

"Sure." Spence picked up a CD and passed it to her. "Have you heard this?"

Carrie read the label. *Fuzzy Squash.* "Yeah, but just a couple of songs," she said. "They had it in one of the listening stations last week. It's not that good."

"Too bad," Spence said. "Their first album really rocked."

"Yeah, I heard the second one was pretty good, too," Carrie said, "but I haven't been able to find it here."

Spence leaned closer. "Mall stores never have the best selection," he confided. "There's this place down on Fifth Street, though—near the skate park? It's called Beat of a Different Drummer, and they have tons of stuff. Fewer of the mainstream hits and more bands like Medusa and Safe Zone."

Carrie's eyes widened. "I've been looking for the Safe Zone CD for so long," she said.

"They've got it," Spence told her. "If you ever pick it up, stop by the skate park afterward. Matt and I are there all the time, and I usually have a portable stereo. We could pop it in."

"Cool," Carrie said.

"Carrie!" Theresa and Anna called, running up to her at the same time.

"I told you she'd be here," Theresa said to Anna, and Anna handed her a quarter.

"I guessed food court," Anna said with a shrug. "But anyway . . . how was your first rehearsal?"

"Yeah—tell us all about it," Theresa said.

Carrie grimaced. "It started out bad and got worse," she said.

"Really? What happened?" Theresa asked. Carrie didn't feel much like talking about it, so she looked to Spence for help.

"It's like this," Spence said. "We gave the lines a try, but my rhyming didn't fly, we had Scooby standing by, splashin' water in my eye; we wiped the table dry, Mrs. W. wanted to cry, and when Matt came boarding in, I thought she was gonna die."

Carrie laughed. It was a pretty accurate description, although Anna and Theresa looked totally confused.

"Someone want to explain that again?" Theresa asked. "In English?"

Carrie shook her head. "Not really," she said.

"Oh, come on—it couldn't have been that bad," Anna prodded.

"It was," Carrie said. Her friends looked at her with disbelief. "I'm serious," Carrie insisted. "First I yelled all my lines and spilled water all over the table. Then I was so upset about messing up that I couldn't get any of my lines out. I stuttered through everything in a really quiet voice, and it was so bad that Mrs. Wessex dismissed us early. We didn't even finish the read through."

"Yikes," Anna said.

"Double yikes," Carrie agreed. "It was so bad, I don't even think I should go back tomorrow." She looked at Spence. "You guys would probably be better off without me."

"No way, Scoob—you're the only one that laughs at my rhymes."

Carrie cocked her head. "That's not true," she said. "Everyone laughs at your rhymes."

"Not Mrs. W.," Spence said.

Carrie winced. "Yeah, she doesn't really seem to like it all that much," she told Theresa and Anna.

"Too bad," Theresa said. "I liked the idea of having an emcee instead of a narrator."

"Yeah, I think it works," Anna agreed.

"Me too," said Spence. "I'm going to go home and write up more new lines for tomorrow."

Carrie raised her eyebrows. "You're going to keep doing it?" she asked.

"Yeah, why not?" Spence said. "I gotta be me, and Mrs. W. will come around."

Carrie wasn't so sure about that. "You really think so?"

"Sure," Spence said. "And if she doesn't, what's the worst that can happen? I'll have to do the lines straight up and be boring for a few nights. I can cope."

Wow, Carrie thought. Spence seemed so cool about it all—like it was no big deal. If only she could be that relaxed about the play. Then maybe she'd be able to say her lines without sounding like such a fool. And get up onstage without freezing. And make her dream of becoming an actress come true.

Right, Carrie thought. *And maybe Sharon will apologize for giving me all that bad advice.*

Nope. After today's rehearsal it seemed pretty clear. She wasn't the natural actress that she'd thought she was, and the sooner she gave up on that dream, the better it would be—for everyone.

CHAPTER
Nine

"Carrie—you'd better get up! You're going to be late for school!"

Carrie lay in bed, staring at the glow-in-the-dark moon and stars stickers on her ceiling. She'd gotten them for her seventh birthday and still remembered how cool she'd thought they were.

Just then the door to Carrie's bedroom swung open, and her mom stood there, her arms crossed over her chest. "Your father made you soy pancakes and they're getting cold," she said.

Great—more soy products. Luckily, Lynn had been sneaking her cherry Pop-Tarts on the car ride to school. But not today. Lynn had left early for some kind of college fair. Not that it mattered. Carrie wasn't planning on going to school anyway.

"I don't feel well," she moaned. "I think I'm coming down with something."

Ms. Weingarten rushed over and put her hand on Carrie's forehead. She frowned. "You do feel a little warm," she said. "Let me get the thermometer."

She was back in two seconds and popped the thermometer into Carrie's mouth. Carrie tried to think warm thoughts while they waited for the thermometer to beep. *Summer,* she told herself. *Barbecues, blackflies, mosquitoes.* Finally, the thermometer sounded, and Carrie's mom took it out.

"Hmmm, ninety-eight point eight," Ms. Weingarten said. "That's not much of a fever."

"Yeah, but my stomach really hurts," Carrie said quickly. "Maybe there was something wrong with that casserole Dad made last night." With her father's cooking, food poisoning was always a possibility.

"He *did* use a lot of high-fiber grains," Carrie's mom muttered. "Really, I wouldn't mind if your father calmed down a bit from this *healthy* diet." She shook her head. "I have to admit, lately my stomach's been feeling a little uneasy, too."

"So can I stay home, then?" Carrie asked hopefully. If she could get out of play practice for just one day, she was sure it would run more smoothly without her. Then maybe Mrs. Wessex would be more inclined to let her quit when she asked.

"Well, if your stomach's *really* bothering you—"

A loud crash interrupted her mom, and Carrie looked over to see her backpack on the floor, papers spilled everywhere. Right on top was the bright pink sheet with the rehearsal schedule for the play. A glance at the desk chair where her backpack had been confirmed what Carrie had already suspected. Bob stood on the edge of the chair, looking down at her work with pride.

"How did that happen?" Ms. Weingarten said, walking over to pick up the papers. Without thinking, Carrie jumped out of bed and dashed over to grab the rehearsal schedule before her mom could see it.

"Carrie, you're—what are you doing?" her mom asked. She looked at Carrie with confusion, and then slowly her features transformed into her mom face. Her eyes got all scrunched together and her lips formed a tight line. "Carrie, what's on that piece of paper?" she asked, her voice firm.

Slowly, Carrie handed it over.

"Aha," Ms. Weingarten said, scanning the schedule. "Today is your second rehearsal for the play. Well, you sure got out of bed fast for someone with a horrible stomachache."

Carrie looked down at the floor, feeling bad for lying to her mom. "You don't understand, Mom. I really messed up yesterday. I can't go back. They're better off without me there. Really."

"Carrie, I know you're nervous," her mom said. "But you made a commitment to take this role, and you have to follow through."

Carrie glared at Bob. Stupid unicorn. Now she'd never be able to quit. Even if Mrs. Wessex was willing to let her, her mother never would.

"Don't you need a nap?" Carrie asked as she headed toward Mrs. Hendrickson's room that afternoon.

"Nope," Bob said. She had demanded that Carrie let her ride on her shoulder again, like she had at the mall, because riding in the backpack made her sleepy, and she wanted to stay awake through this rehearsal.

"Are you sure?" Carrie asked. "Because I think you might be getting bags under your eyes."

"Really?" the little unicorn gasped. Then she looked up at Carrie and grinned. "Nice try," she said, "but I'm coming with you. And I'm staying awake. You're going to go in there today and knock 'em dead. Trust me."

Carrie snorted. "Why should I? So far you've stolen my journal, shown pages of it to my teacher, whined until I bought you all kinds of stupid jewelry and hair stuff, and ratted me out to my mom."

"All for your own good," Bob said.

Carrie groaned. "Yeah, well, do me a favor and don't do me any more favors, okay?"

"Believe in yourself and I'll leave you alone," Bob said. Then she jumped off Carrie's shoulder and pranced into Mrs. Hendrickson's room.

"Where are you—?" Carrie started, but Lauren and Maria were coming, so she had to just let Bob go.

"Hey, Carrie, did you practice your lines?" Sharon asked when she saw Carrie walk in.

Carrie nodded. She'd wolfed down her lunch so that she could spend the rest of the period, along with study hall, reading over her lines and song lyrics.

"Well, you better take a look at this," Sharon said, passing her a piece of paper.

"What is it?"

"An e-mail Mrs. Wessex sent me last night.

She asked me to forward it to you, too, but I don't have your e-mail address."

"What do you mean, you don't have my address?" Carrie asked. "You e-mail me all the time."

"I know, but I loaded some new software the other day, and I guess it erased part of my address book. Anyway, take a look at the note."

Carrie squinted at Sharon, not quite sure what to make of her whole e-mail excuse. It certainly didn't sound legitimate. The e-mail itself, however, looked real.

Dear Sharon and Carrie—

    After yesterday's rehearsal, I
decided to make a few changes. Sharon, I
would like you to play the part of Cindy
Rellar, and Carrie, I would like you to
take over as Rae Punzille. I believe
that Mrs. Hendrickson and I miscast the
two of you to begin with and that everyone will benefit from this simple
change. Please study your new lines and
be ready to practice your duet—with
Sharon as Cindy and Carrie as Rae—first
thing at practice tomorrow afternoon.

                    Sincerely,
                    Mrs. Wessex

P.S. Sharon, could you please forward this e-mail to Carrie? I don't have her address.

Carrie blinked and read the note over again. "I—I don't get it," she said. "Why would Mrs. Wessex do this? And why would she just tell you and not me?"

"She has my home e-mail because my mom is part of the Booster Club, but she doesn't have yours. And like I said," Sharon continued, "I would have forwarded it to you, but I couldn't find your address."

Carrie frowned. "But . . . why would she send an e-mail? Why didn't she just tell us in class today or something?"

"You're kidding, right?" Sharon asked. She glanced around, then lowered her voice. "You were practically in tears when you left rehearsal yesterday. She probably didn't dare to tell you in person. You get embarrassed so easily, she probably just thought e-mail would be safer."

"I don't know, Sharon," Carrie said. She skimmed the note again. It did sound like Mrs. Wessex's writing, but Carrie didn't dare to believe what Sharon was saying. What if it was just another trick? *Or worse,* Carrie thought, *what if it isn't?*

What if Mrs. Wessex really had switched their

parts? But that didn't sound like something Mrs. Wessex would do—at least not through an e-mail.

Carrie held the note out to Sharon. "I don't buy it," she said. "You're just trying to make me—"

"Carrie? Sharon? Could you come over here, please?" Mrs. Wessex called.

Sharon glowered at Carrie and snatched the paper out of her hand. "Coming," she called, and she headed over to the piano. Carrie followed her cautiously, still wondering about the e-mail and whether it could possibly be true.

"Since we have Mrs. Hendrickson here, I'd like to start out with your duet today," Mrs. Wessex said. "Carrie—did Sharon tell you about the changes I made?"

"The—? You—?" Carrie stared at Sharon in disbelief. Sharon grinned. "She . . . um . . ." It was true. The e-mail had been real. Mrs. Wessex really had switched their roles. And after only one rehearsal.

"Carrie?" Mrs. Wessex asked, furrowing her brow.

"I, uh . . ." Suddenly, Carrie felt like the whole room was spinning. Her face was hot, her arms were tingling, and she felt like she was going to throw up. "I don't feel well," she managed finally. Then she turned and sprinted for the door.

"Carrie?" she heard Mrs. Wessex call, but she wasn't stopping for anything. Carrie kept running until she was outside where she could take deep breaths of the fresh cool air.

"Hey, Scoob—what's up?" Spence called as he rushed out the door.

"Nothing," Carrie said. She wasn't about to explain the situation to Spence or to anyone else. It was too humiliating. Let them hear it from Mrs. Wessex. Or Sharon. "I just—I feel really sick all of a sudden. Can you tell Mrs. Wessex I had to leave?"

"Sure thing," Spence said. "See you tomorrow."

Yeah, Carrie thought, *but probably not at play rehearsal.* After all, it had only taken Mrs. Wessex one play rehearsal to cut Carrie's lines back. After today, she'd probably eliminate Carrie altogether.

CHAPTER
Ten

"Why did you run off like that?" Bob demanded back in Carrie's room.

"Glad to see you were so on top of things today," Carrie said sarcastically. "Thanks for looking out for me."

Bob jumped up onto Carrie's pillow and stared her in the eyes. "Would you cut it out already? I said I was sorry—I just got side-tracked in the prop room. There were all these mirrors. . . ."

Carrie exhaled sharply and rolled over to face the other way. But Bob wouldn't give up. She jumped onto Carrie's head and ran down her cheek onto the pillow so that they were face-to-face again.

"What happened?" she repeated.

"Mrs. Wessex switched me and Sharon. Now

I'm supposed to play Rae, and Sharon's playing Cindy."

Bob snorted and shook her mane. "That doesn't make sense. Why would she do that?"

"Because she doesn't want me to wreck the play."

"Did she say that?" Bob asked.

"No."

"Well, what did she say?"

"Nothing," Carrie said.

"So then . . . how do you know she switched your parts?"

Carrie sighed. "Sharon told me. Mrs. Wessex sent her an e-mail last night, and Sharon showed it to me right before rehearsal."

"That sounds kind of sketchy to me," Bob said.

"I thought so, too," Carrie said, "but then Mrs. Wessex asked me if Sharon had told me about the changes, so I figured it was true."

"Hmmm," Bob grunted. "I don't like the sound of this." She pranced back and forth a few times, tossing her mane, then came to a stop. "Here's what you're going to do. Get—"

"Aaagh!" Carrie groaned. "There's nothing for me to do. I'm a bad actress, and I'm never going to get any better. Would you stop trying to help me?"

Bob stared at her for a moment. "Yes," she said. "But only on one condition. You get Anna and Theresa on the phone and tell them what happened this afternoon. You do that, and I'll leave you alone. Okay?"

Carrie narrowed her eyes at the little unicorn. "Okay," she said. And she grabbed the phone.

One hour later Carrie, Theresa, and Anna were on their way into Access Café on Main Street in Newcastle.

"There's an open computer over there," Anna pointed out. Carrie and Theresa followed her, and they pulled up three chairs in front of the monitor.

"Thanks for the ride," Bob whispered into Carrie's ear. "Don't leave without me."

Carrie felt Bob hopping off her shoulder and watched the unicorn trot off to another free computer in the back corner of the café. True to her word, Bob had left Carrie alone ever since she'd gotten off the phone with Theresa and Anna. Now her friends were the ones who wouldn't let the whole Sharon role-switching thing go.

"I still don't believe Mrs. Wessex sent Sharon that e-mail," Anna said. "I wish you'd stayed for the duet. Then we'd know exactly what changes

Mrs. Wessex was talking about. I'm sure it wasn't anything like what Sharon told you."

Carrie sighed. "I don't know. It makes sense," she said. "I did okay in the audition, but I was terrible at the rehearsal yesterday, and I *was* practically in tears. Mrs. Wessex probably figured I'd be happy to switch parts with Sharon. Rae does have fewer lines. And Cindy is supposed to start the whole play off with a solo. Mrs. Wessex probably just realized there was no way I could pull that off."

"Carrie, cut it out," Theresa said. "You're being way too hard on yourself. For one thing, you were better than okay at the audition—you were *great*."

"And you could definitely pull off the solo," Anna added. "You have an amazing voice—way better than Sharon's."

"Thanks," Carrie said, but she was sure her friends were just being nice. "So . . . why are we here, anyway?"

"To check out Sharon's story," Anna said. "It'll be easier to do here because there's a faster Internet connection. See, first we need to find out Mrs. Wessex's e-mail address. I'm sure she's listed as one of the contacts on the ECS home page, so we can get it from there. Then—"

"Hey, Anna," Theresa interrupted. "Isn't that Mrs. Wessex over there?"

Carrie looked over at the entrance to the café and groaned. "Oh, no. I can't let her see me," she said. "I asked Spence to tell her I was sick!"

"Okay, just try to sit a little lower," Theresa said, "and she won't see you over the monitor."

"What if I go talk to her?" Anna suggested. "I can make sure she sits with her back to us." Without waiting for an answer, Anna jumped up and hurried over to their teacher, who was just starting to look around the café for a spot.

Carrie hunkered down in her chair but tried to peek out enough to watch what happened. She saw Anna talking to Mrs. Wessex, carefully steering her to the other side of the café.

"Isn't she awesome?" Theresa asked Carrie.

"Yeah, she's brave," Carrie agreed.

In a minute Anna was back, and her brown eyes were lit up with excitement. "You guys won't believe this," she said as she sat down next to Carrie. "I knew it! I knew I was right."

"About what?" Theresa asked.

"Listen to this." Anna focused her gaze on Carrie. "Mrs. Wessex just told me that she doesn't usually come here, but she had to because her computer at home isn't working, and she hasn't been able to check her e-mail in three days."

Anna sat back and folded her arms across her chest.

"Oh, my gosh," Theresa began. "That means . . ."

"There's no way she could have sent that e-mail to Sharon!" Anna said. "See? I *knew* Sharon was lying."

"Well, then what did Mrs. Wessex mean when she asked me if Sharon had told me about the *changes*?" Carrie asked.

"I don't know," Anna said. "But it was probably just something small that Sharon blew way out of proportion to upset you."

Carrie shook her head. She'd done it again. She'd fallen for one of Sharon's tricks and let it ruin another whole day of rehearsal.

"Don't worry, Carrie," Anna said. "We'll find a way to get her back."

"Yeah," Theresa said. "You just go home and relax. Work on memorizing your lines or something. Anna and I will come up with a plan to put Sharon in her place."

"Ooh, I can't wait for school tomorrow," Bob said when she and Carrie were back in Carrie's room. They were on Carrie's bed, in the middle of Bob's one hundred brush strokes, since Carrie hadn't gotten a chance to do them at school that day. "What do you think Theresa and Anna are going to do?" Bob asked.

"I don't know," Carrie said. "I'm trying not to think about it too much. Every time I realize that I fell for another one of Sharon's stupid tricks, it makes me want to—"

"Hey, easy on the mane," Bob yelled out.

"Sorry," Carrie said, realizing she'd been brushing kind of hard. She loosened her grip on the toothbrush and finished the last five strokes. "It just makes me so mad."

"Then you're right—you shouldn't think about it," Bob said, admiring her mane. "Besides, we've got other business tonight."

"We do?" Carrie asked.

"Yep," Bob told her with twinkling eyes. "Take a look in your backpack," she said.

Carrie laid down the toothbrush and went to open up her bag. A bunch of computer paper spilled out with the Access Café logo on top.

"What's all this?" Carrie asked. She read the heading at the top of the page. " 'Tips on getting over stage fright'?"

"It took me a while," Bob said. "I had to type one key at a time with my horn! But I finally managed to spell out *stage fright* at Google, and it came up with all this cool stuff."

"Wow," Carrie said, looking at the little unicorn with newfound appreciation. "That was actually a really good idea, Bob."

"Don't look so surprised," Bob said indignantly.

Carrie chuckled, scooping up the unicorn as she walked back to her desk and sat down to read through the papers.

"'Tips for getting over stage fright,'" she read aloud. "'Number one: Picture the audience in their underwear.'"

"Ew!" she and Bob both screeched at the same time.

"What's the next one?" Bob asked.

"'Number two: When memorizing your lines, practice them out loud—not just in your head.'"

"Sounds good," Bob said. "Keep going."

"'Number three: Read through your lines outside of rehearsals with a friend who is not in the play. Your friend will be more focused on you than the other characters' lines and therefore more able to offer you feedback.'"

"Not bad," Bob said. "What else is there?"

Carrie flipped through the pages, soaking in all of the advice. She especially liked the tip about pretending that she was just having a real conversation with someone, as her character, and no one else was watching. That was kind of how it had felt in the audition when she was arguing with Sharon and Kimberly about Cindy going to the prom.

"Hey, what's this?" Carrie asked when she got to the last page. She scrunched up her nose. The stuff on that page didn't have anything to do with stage fright—it was some article out of a parenting magazine.

"Oh, that . . . How'd that get in there?" Bob asked, tilting her head.

"'Unique names for girls'?" Carrie read. *"Bob—"*

"Huh. That one must have got mixed in with my stuff by accident," the little unicorn said, shifting from one side to the other. "But you know, since we have it . . . maybe we should take a look at it. It might be interesting."

"Mm-hm," Carrie said. "Mixed in by accident, huh?"

"I swear," Bob said, her eyes twinkling.

"I bet," Carrie muttered. But she scanned the article anyway. "All right. How about Katherina?"

"I'd have to wear a tutu."

"Esther?"

"Sounds like a hen."

"Nanette?"

"Too prissy."

"Molly?"

"That's a lapdog."

"Regina?"

"Vacuum cleaner."

"Clementine?"

"You want to name me after a fruit?"

"*Bob!*" Carrie yelled.

The unicorn snorted and stamped her feet. "Yeah, I guess you're right," she said finally. "That's the only name that seems to fit. Fine. Forget the list. Bob it is. Now go get your script—you've got some lines to learn!"

CHAPTER
Eleven

Carrie nibbled at her egg-free egg-salad sandwich, watching the cafeteria line for Sharon. She
and Anna and Theresa had been at the lunch
table for a few minutes already, and Carrie was
so anxious, she could barely eat. They'd told
Carrie that morning that they were going to
spring their "trap" for Sharon at lunchtime—
but they'd been totally mysterious about what
they were going to do.

"Hey, there she is," Theresa said.

Sharon and Kimberly walked out of the line
together, then headed straight for their table and
sat down.

"Hey, Carrie, do you think you'll make it
through rehearsal today?" Kimberly asked. She
smirked at Sharon.

"Yep, I'll be there," Carrie said. "Actually, I

even learned most of my lines last night. And the lyrics to the songs, too."

Bob, who was resting on Carrie's shoulder, gave her a proud little poke.

"That reminds me, Sharon," Anna said, sounding supercasual. "Did Mrs. Wessex send you any more e-mails?"

Sharon looked at Carrie, narrowing her eyes. "No," she said. "Why?"

Anna shrugged. "Well, I got one from her last night. She needed me to know some stuff about the set design. She said we didn't need as many chairs at the prom because she's decided Rae isn't going to be there."

"What? Why not?" Sharon demanded. "That's the biggest scene in the whole play. Rae has to be there."

"That's what I thought at first, too," Theresa said. "But then I thought about it and realized that the play's really about Cindy, you know? I mean, Rae's just a supporting character. No one's really going to miss her if she doesn't go to the dance."

"Rae is not a supporting character!" Sharon hissed. "She's just as big a role as Cindy. Of course people are going to notice if she's not there."

Anna shrugged again. "Well, that's the way Mrs. Wessex wants it."

"That doesn't make sense," Sharon said. Her face was so red, it rivaled Carrie's hair. "She can't cut Rae out of the last scene."

"Sure, she can," Theresa said. "It's her play—she wrote it."

Carrie had to bite her lip to keep a straight face. She watched her friends with amazement. Sharon was totally losing it, but Theresa and Anna were perfectly calm.

"And just when was she going to tell me about it?" Sharon asked.

"I don't know," Anna said. "Probably today at rehearsal. After all, it's not like it really affects you."

"Of course it affects me!" Sharon yelled. "She's cutting me out of the last scene—she's taking away my solo."

"Oh, no," Theresa said. She touched Sharon's arm as if she were trying to comfort her. "She's not cutting *your* part—she's cutting *Carrie's*. The two of you switched roles, right?"

"Yeah, Carrie told us all about it," Anna said. "She's playing Rae now, and you're Cindy."

"We—" Sharon started. "I—" she tried again. But she couldn't go any further. Theresa and

Anna had executed their plan perfectly, and now she was trapped. She grabbed hold of her lunch tray and stood up. "I'm going to go talk to Mrs. Wessex," she said. "Come on, Kimberly." Like the loyal lackey that she was, Kimberly stood and followed Sharon out of the cafeteria.

"All right!" Theresa, Anna, and Carrie all shouted when she was gone, slapping each other high fives.

"That was beautiful, you two," Carrie said.

"Thanks," Theresa said. "It was mostly Anna's idea. She can be really sneaky when she needs to be. I'm glad she's on our side."

"There's no other side I'd rather be on," Anna said.

"So . . . what do we do now?" Carrie asked.

"Nothing," Anna said. "We just let Sharon figure out that we tricked her and that will be that."

"Do you think she'll try to trick me again?" Carrie asked.

"Uh-uh." Anna shook her head. "From what I've seen, Sharon only bites until someone bites back."

"And she definitely just got bitten," Carrie said.

★   ★   ★

"I can't believe it's almost midnight."

"Me neither. But I think we have time for one last dance before you have to go."

Carrie smiled at Matt, feeling like she really was Cindy Rellar at the prom with the boy of her dreams.

"Beautiful!" Mrs. Wessex declared. "Wonderful job, all of you. And now we'll work on the final song."

Rehearsal that afternoon had been amazing. Carrie had followed the tips Bob had gotten online—except for the one about picturing people in their underwear—and she'd barely messed up at all. It really helped that she had most of her lines memorized now. And Sharon hadn't been acting up, either—though *Rae* hadn't looked too happy when Cindy and Charlie Prinze had their dance.

"Matthew, you can leave your skateboard over there," Mrs. Wessex instructed as everyone moved over to the piano. She'd finally caved and allowed him to use the board—but only when he arrived at the prom, and only if he promised not to try any "fancy stunts." She'd even decided that Spence could rap his lines since he really was showing a lot of "initiative" and "creativity."

Now came the final test—would Carrie sound okay during her duet with Sharon?

Mrs. Hendrickson played the opening notes, and everyone sang along to the group verse. Then they got to the part where it was just Carrie and Sharon.

Closing her eyes, Carrie continued to sing, trying not to think about anything but the music. She'd gone over the lyrics so many times with Bob that she could picture them in her head. And every time she started to feel nervous, she just pretended she was singing along with the car radio. Tip number twenty-two.

When it was Sharon's turn to sing by herself, Carrie opened her eyes and waited, twisting her hands together. And when her part came around, she was ready.

"Everything must end," Carrie sang, all by herself. *"But even so, at least now I know, I have what I need—a real, true friend."*

The rest of the cast joined in for the final verse of the song, and then they were done.

Carrie felt a burst of pride—she'd done it! She'd made it through the entire rehearsal without getting freaked out. She could feel Bob jumping around on her shoulder, and she knew the unicorn was just as excited.

"Nice work, everyone," Mrs. Hendrickson said.

"Yes, I'm very pleased with how hard you've all been working," Mrs. Wessex added. "And just think—in a week you'll get to perform for a real audience. Imagine how exciting that will be!"

Carrie gulped. She'd been so focused on doing okay in rehearsal that somehow she'd forgotten that she still had to do this in front of other people. Bob and her friends had helped her make it this far, but what if she fell apart when it really mattered?

CHAPTER
Twelve

"I still don't get it," Carrie said as she carefully put Bob's earring chokers around the little unicorn's neck. "Why do *you* need to get dressed up for *my* play?"

Bob sighed. "Just put on my anklet, would you?"

Carrie took the open-ended rhinestone ring and slid it over Bob's hoof, tightening it so it would stay in place. "There—you look beautiful," she said.

"Really?"

"Yes, really," Carrie said. "But what about this?" She picked up the green butterfly hair clip.

"That," Bob said, "is for you."

Carrie started to protest, then tilted her head and stared at her reflection in the mirror. This *was* a special occasion, and her bangs were still hanging in her face, even though her mother had tried to curl them out of the way.

"Go for it!" Bob said with a grin.

Before she could change her mind, Carrie pulled her hair back and cinched the clip in place. It actually looked okay. And it did feel nice to have her hair off her forehead. Not to mention the fact that she could see a lot more clearly.

"Awesome—you're going to knock 'em dead," Bob said. "Just remember everything we talked about. And if you have to, use that 'picture the crowd in their underwear' trick. But only as a last resort."

Carrie laughed in spite of her nerves. "Okay," she said. "Only as a last resort."

She carried Bob out of the bathroom and walked down to the auditorium. Somehow tonight, with all the lights and the people milling around, it looked bigger than it had during rehearsals. But Carrie tried not to think about it too much. Instead she walked over to the piano and set Bob in a flower arrangement there. The little unicorn had insisted it would be the perfect place to watch from. Then Carrie went backstage and joined the rest of the cast.

"Carrie, you look great!" Kimberly said when she saw her. Theresa had picked out matching boot-cut black pants and V-necked shirts for Cindy and Rae to wear. All they had to do was change into dresses for the prom scene.

"Thanks," Carrie said. "You, um . . . you look good, too."

Kimberly's stepmom costume wasn't really as cool as what Carrie and Sharon got to wear. She was stuck in a loose dress with big tacky flowers all over it. But at least she did look like she could be somebody's mother.

"Hey, Carrie, can I talk to you for a sec?" Sharon asked.

Carrie frowned. "I guess so," she said.

They hadn't really talked much since the scene in the cafeteria the week before—just enough to get through rehearsals. And that had been fine with Carrie. The less time she spent thinking about Sharon, the better.

Carrie followed Sharon back to the prop room.

"So, I just wanted to say—um, break a leg," Sharon said.

Carrie scowled at her. "I can't believe you. Here I thought you were going to apologize, and you go and say something mean." She turned to leave.

"No, wait!" Sharon said, grabbing her arm. "You don't understand—'break a leg' is what actors say before a performance. It's just an expression. It means 'good luck.'"

Carrie eyed Sharon suspiciously. "Oh. Well . . . is that all you wanted to say? *Good luck?*"

Sharon nodded. "That and . . . well, that I'm sorry I was . . . I mean, I'm sorry I didn't . . . I know you'll do a good job tonight, Carrie," she said finally. For once she actually looked sincere. It wasn't an apology, exactly, but Carrie knew it was probably the best Sharon could do.

"Thanks," Carrie said. "You too."

"All right, then," Sharon said, tossing her long hair behind her shoulder. "Are you ready to show everyone just how good we are?"

"Ready."

They rejoined the rest of the group, and Mrs. Wessex went out onstage to let the audience know they were ready to begin.

Theresa and Anna had already been backstage getting some of the props ready, and as soon as they saw Carrie, they rushed over to her.

"Hey, how do you feel?" Theresa asked.

"The truth?" Carrie winced. "I'm *so* nervous."

"You'll be fine," Anna reassured her.

"Better than fine," Theresa added, squeezing Carrie's hand. "You'll be great!"

"Thanks, guys."

Hearing her friends' encouragement helped, but right then Carrie couldn't imagine how she was going to hear anyone's lines over her heart pounding its way straight out of her chest.

"Five minutes until curtain call," Mrs. Wessex sang out.

"Hey, Scoob!"

Carrie turned around and saw Spence standing there. His costume looked pretty much like what he wore to school every day, which was fitting since he seemed to be playing himself. Mrs. Wessex had even let him call his character MC Spence.

"Are you ready?" Carrie asked.

"Sure," Spence said with a shrug.

Carrie squinted at him. "Are you nervous?" she asked.

Spence mulled the question over for a minute. "Well," he said, "my heart's beating double time, my head's filling up with rhyme, my pulse continues to climb, but this feeling—it is sublime."

"So . . . a little bit?" Carrie said with a grin.

"Yeah, a little bit," Spence said. "But it's all good. The adrenaline just means you're ready, right?"

Carrie shook her head. He was too much. "Yeah. Ready," she said, "but not steady . . . Freddie."

Spence winced. "We'll work on that," he said, and Carrie laughed.

"Places, everyone!" Mrs. Wessex called. "We're ready for the curtain."

Mrs. Wessex began ushering everyone to their spots, and before she knew it, Carrie was out there onstage, ready to begin her solo. She heard Mrs. Hendrickson start in on the piano, and as the curtain parted, Carrie came in right on cue.

"I dream of a day all my own," she sang. *"With no work to be done."* From the wings she saw Spence, Anna, and Theresa all giving her thumbs-up. In the flower arrangement she could see Bob shaking her mane from side to side.

And before she knew it, her song was over and the audience was clapping. It was an amazing feeling, knowing that the applause was for her, and suddenly she understood what Spence had said about the adrenaline.

Her heart was pounding and her arms were tingling, but she didn't feel scared anymore. She just felt excited . . . and ready.

"I want everyone to know how proud we are of you," Mrs. Wessex said later that night.

The cast was assembled in Mrs. Hendrickson's

room, where they'd met up after changing out of their costumes. In a few minutes Carrie would be heading out to Ed's Soda Shop at the mall with her friends to celebrate, but right now she was just basking in the moment.

The final curtain call had been amazing. The cast had come on in groups, and the audience had applauded all of them. But when Carrie, Sharon, Matt, and Spence had come out for their final bow, the applause had picked up even more, until it sounded like thunder. And then the audience had actually stood up and given them a standing ovation.

Now that it was over, Carrie couldn't help noticing that the whole night had felt like a dream. A really good dream. *A flying dream.* And as nervous as she'd been at the beginning of the night, she was ten times more excited to come out and do it again tomorrow night.

"Yes, you all did a wonderful job," Mrs. Hendrickson added. "Great work!"

"And don't forget," Mrs. Wessex said, "we're meeting here tomorrow at 6 P.M. to get ready for the next show. Tonight was wonderful, but I have a feeling tomorrow night is going to be even better. Thank you, everyone."

Everybody clapped and cheered, still buzzing

with excitement from having pulled off their first performance without a hitch. Eventually, though, people drifted off to go find their families and friends.

Carrie headed back to the auditorium and went straight to the floral arrangement. "Did you see, Bob?" she whispered as she got close. "I did it! I starred in the school play and I didn't even mess up. It was so much fun! I can hardly wait for—" Carrie looked at the flowers. "Bob?" she called out softly.

There was no response.

Frowning, Carrie spread a few of the stems apart so she could see the edge of the basket better. Then she stuck her hand straight into the green flora foam and felt around. After a few moments of searching, she brought her hand back out and examined the things she'd found. A hoop earring, a rhinestone ring, and a small, silver unicorn.

"Bob," Carrie whispered, staring at the charm in her hand. All at once a lump formed in her throat. It was funny. As annoying as the little unicorn had been at times, Carrie had really gotten used to having her around. It was hard to believe that it had been less than two weeks since she'd first found her under the water fountain.

Carrie thought about their first meeting and

tried to remember exactly what it was the little unicorn had told her. Something about a few people on her side of the universe thinking that Carrie needed encouragement. And she definitely had. But now it seemed Bob's job was over, and it was time for her to go back to . . . her side of the universe, wherever that was.

Carrie looked up to the lights and smiled. "Thanks, Bob," she said softly. Then she looked down at the charm and laughed. The second hoop earring—one of Bob's chokers—had remained around her neck when she'd turned back into a charm. *She'd like that*, Carrie thought. *Permanent jewelry.*

But what was even neater about the earring was the way it had twisted around at the top, forming a perfect loop. Carrie took one look at it and knew exactly what it was meant for.

She unclasped the charm bracelet that Anna had given her and slid the unicorn charm on next to the angel one that had been on it originally.

"You make a nice pair," Carrie said to the two charms, and just for a second she could have sworn she saw Bob's eyes twinkle—just a little.

Get Ready for Charm Club
Book #3:
fairy

"Theresa!" Mrs. Allen called. "Carrie and Anna are here!"

Theresa came running down the staircase to meet her friends. They were planning to walk over to the school together for the final performance of *Cindy Rellar*—the Sunday matinee.

"Hi, Resa," Carrie said. "Ready?"

"Almost. I just have to find my shoes." Theresa rummaged around in the bottom of the coat closet, but she came out empty-handed. "Just a sec," she told her friends. "Hey, Mom?" she shouted.

"I'm right here, Theresa. No need to yell," Mrs. Allen said, walking into the foyer.

"Oh, sorry," Theresa replied. "Have you seen my sneakers?"

Theresa's mother pressed her lips together

and thought. "In the living room?" she suggested.

"I'll check," Theresa said, running off. A few moments later she was back, holding a sneaker in each hand. "Found 'em. Thanks, Mom," she said.

"I thought I'd seen them in there. Maybe I should get you some kind of beeper to attach to the laces so you can find them more easily," Mrs. Allen said with a laugh.

"That'd be cool," Theresa said, playing along with the joke. "But you'd have to get me one for my backpack, too. And my jacket. And my school notebook and my key chain and my wallet."

"Okay, I'll look into it," Mrs. Allen called over her shoulder as she headed toward the kitchen.

"Beepers would be nice," Theresa said. "Or maybe something with flashing lights. I do misplace stuff a lot." She walked toward the bench next to the staircase, juggling her sneakers as she went.

"Hey, Resa," Carrie said. "That's pretty good the way you can cross them in midair. Can you juggle three?"

"I think so," Theresa said. She picked up a shoe that belonged to her little brother, Nick, and added it to the mix. For a minute she was able to keep all three of them in the air—until she tossed Nick's shoe a little too hard. It sailed up over the banister and knocked a framed picture of Theresa's grandparents off the wall.

"Oh no!" Theresa cried over the tinkling of broken glass.

"Theresa?" her mother called, rushing back in. "What happened?"

"I was, um . . . trying to juggle," Theresa said, staring down at her toes.

"Juggle what?" Mrs. Allen asked.

"Sneakers."

"In the house?"

"Well . . ." Theresa hesitated. Somehow "yes" didn't seem like a very good answer.

Mrs. Allen looked from the shoes in Theresa's hands to the tiny sneaker on the staircase and back again.

"I'm really sorry, Mom," Theresa said. "I'll clean it up."

"No." Her mother shook her head. "Don't worry about it. You girls need to get over to the school. I'll take care of this."

"I'm really sorry," Theresa said again. "I didn't mean to."

Mrs. Allen's face softened and she looked straight into Theresa's eyes. "Of course you didn't. It was an accident. And besides, it's only a picture frame—it can be replaced. The important thing is that no one was hurt, right?"

"Right," Theresa said with a sigh. Then she turned to Carrie and Anna. "Come on. I can put these on outside." She led her friends through the front door and sat down heavily on the top step of the porch. "There," she said when she had finished tying the laces. "I'm ready."

"Cool," Anna said. "But don't forget the flowers."

Theresa narrowed her eyes. "What flowers?"

"The ones you were supposed to pick up for Mrs. Wessex. You know—the bouquet we're giving her after the final performance?"

Theresa's jaw dropped open. "Oh, no! Anna! I totally forgot!"

"Oh," Anna said, raising her eyebrows. "Well . . . that's okay. I'm sure we can pick something up on the way."

Theresa slumped back onto the porch and put her head in her hands. "I am such an idiot," she said.

"Resa," Carrie said, "don't be so hard on yourself. It's not a big deal. We'll just grab some on the way like Anna said. That florist right next to the bakery always has nice arrangements."

"That's not the point," Theresa said unhappily.

"Those flowers are like the eighteenth thing I've messed up this week."

Anna sat down and put an arm around her friend. "Oh, come on, it can't be that bad."

"Oh yes, it can," Theresa said. "In fact, it's worse. *Way* worse. I've been forgetting stuff and breaking things all over the place. I swear, I'd lose my brain if it wasn't trapped inside my head. Either that or I'd drop it and break it. I'm telling you—I'm a klutz, inside and out."

Wow, Carrie thought. Theresa *was* being really hard on herself. *Just like I was before I got over my stage fright.* Suddenly, Carrie had an idea.

She unclasped the charm bracelet from her wrist and fastened it around her friend's arm. "Here, Theresa," she said.

"What are you doing?" Theresa asked.

Carrie glanced at Anna. "You don't mind, do you, Anna?"

"Not at all," Anna said. "I think it's a great idea."

Theresa held up her arm and examined her new piece of jewelry. "What is it?" she asked.

"It's the charm bracelet that Anna gave me when I messed up my King Tut presentation," Carrie said. "She told me it would bring me good luck, and it did."

"And now we want you to have it," Anna said.

Theresa touched each of the charms and smiled.

"Anna put the angel on there, and I added the unicorn," Carrie told her.

"They're pretty," Theresa said. "Thanks. But don't you want to wear it for the last perform-ance of the play, Carrie?"

Carrie squinted, then shook her head. "I don't think I need it anymore," she said. "And besides, I want you to have it."

"Are you sure?" Theresa asked, gazing up at both of her friends.

"Yep," said Carrie.

"Definitely," said Anna. "I just hope it's as lucky for you as it was for us."

"Yeah," Theresa said with a sigh. "Me too."

WILL A LITTLE CHARM MAGIC BE ENOUGH TO HELP THERESA WITH HER PROBLEM? FIND OUT IN CHARM CLUB BOOK 3: FAIRY